TRUCK
SONG

ANDREW
MACRAE

First published in Australia in November 2013
by Twelfth Planet Press

www.twelfthplanetpress.com

Design and layout by Amanda Rainey
Cover by Kenkichi Tai
Typeset in Sabon MT Pro

National Library of Australia Cataloguing-in-Publication entry

Author: Macrae, Andrew, author.

Title: Trucksong / Andrew Macrae.

ISBN: 9781922101037 (paperback)

Dewey Number: A823.4

For my brother and sister,
fellow travellers in the 1970s trucking-movie childhood

Chapter 1

I clutched at Mum in the crush of bodies and scavenging machines, forest of brown legs dusted by campfire ash and tiers of trucktyre shoes tied with twine. She was heavy with child and me weaned but still a child. We was looking to find a place to lie down but there wasn't no place on that road, no place only for crows in the voices and snatching hands grasping feeling boney arms. And maybe it was me own weight what pulled Mum down, wore her out more than the hollow stomach march and the sandy sinkhole drinking and the sickening and dying all around. She couldn't go no further and there was nowhere to go anyway so we set down by bitumen sweating tar tears and the sunblasted chunks of busted concrete.

The sky split like rotted fruit and darkness came into the nightime shift. Nobody stopped, they all kept on going to wherever they were going. Following food rumours or dowsing rods held upside down by hollow men with sunwracked hands and dry licked lips. But there wasn't nobody to come save them like there was nobody stopping for Mum. And maybe if we were dead they'd be stopping to see what was in our rags worth taking but we weren't dead yet and that babby in Mum's belly started its pains even though looking back I can tell through black blood and matted hair it was birthed too soon. Mum screaming and thrashing, face pulled tight shut and I got the knowing of how dying takes its own time. There's a space in between one shore and the next and I seen Mum in that place all through the long night where time's not counted in minutes or days and I don't want to spend no time there when it's my turn. I want it to be quick.

Daylight dawned and Mum wasn't making no more sounds. I snuggled up against her in the crusted blood blanket while she got colder and colder. We were eyed by a crowd of roaders but they didn't want no part of it, they'd got troubles of their own and pain enough already to share around. And the day warmed up and Mum stiffened, still and quiet, pale blue and cold like the cool clay of a damp creek bed. The crows started gathering, rattling their chests and going *ark arrrrk* and hopping closer. I made noises and flapped my arms but they weren't feared, they'd got my number all right. One hopped up on Mum and looked at me with his white eye and said, 'I know you, boy.'

Just like that, words dropped into my head like stones in a jar. I sat back and the crow ruffled his feathers and flumped his chest and pulled a bloody shred from the blankets. I was frozen in the burning sun, clinging to my frozen Mum.

I laid like that still when a face came out of the dreamy clouds of my tears. Red cheeks above rusty scraggle beard and a weeping sore. Glassy eyes when they seen the child next to its dead Mum.

'You're roadin with me now, cunt.'

I remember it like I remember my own name, the sound of the words as he said them and the sinking feeling in my guts as my whole life changed right there.

He reached out and gave me sips from his skin that I gulped down like sweet nectar though it was only stale water. I saw he had a kid with him then, too, a girl, dark hair, dark eyes, looking low and keeping near her dad. Maybe she saw something in me with them eyes, I dunno, but they bored into me own.

Then he said to the girl, 'Got ourselfs anuvva pair of hands, Isa.'

Wiry arms around me, lifting me up and away from Mum. I felt the scritchy beard and smelled old ganja smoke and rotten-tooth breath and then I was looking back over his shoulder as we walked away and the last thing I seen before sleep took me in its foggy arms was that crow on me Mum and I never forgot it. And that's how I come to be with Smoov and Isa.

In me first memories with Smoov and Isa, the sun was bright and shiny waves falling down from the sky, falling into me eyes to make the tears start. It was a dream like Smoov's shows flickering in me mind, a secret bright box of coloured sound and the blue sparks that flew behind me eyes when he beat me. The look in his face when the clouds came over and he undone his wicked leather belt and said, 'Come ere boy, and take yer punish mint.'

Backhand across me face then onto his knee for the main course. I dunno why he did it. He was stoned and pissed and I got nothing but me fear.

Isa seen what happened and she found me afterwards with smiles and soft voice. She took me hand through the ache and bruises and bloody crying. We walked down to the side of a cool creek through the trees. It was hot and the only sound was the stillness of the air. She washed me in the cold water.

'Where does dreams come from?' I said.

'They is a message come out from the inside to show you anuvva way of thinking on things,' Isa said.

And then that one dream busted open and all that was left was the road and the shattering clatter of steel wheels on tarmac and running light smear in the dark, it's all gone by so fast. I laid down beside Isa beside the creek and I slept in her arms remembering the times I were with Mum and her soft skin touch.

It was the big wet, bugs hummed through shimmering air heavy before the afternoon storm. Clouds on the rim of the gorge, their bright outlines too real, like a false memory. I watched the beatings through half-closed eyes so I didn't have to see them in me sleep. But the memories got in behind me eyes like roadgrit so I didn't know what was true anymore. What was true was the shuddering shivery feeling in me guts when I looked at Isa and I saw the red dirt of those warm lazy days and sap dripping in the sun, billabong bright and clear and the broken ridge above. It didn't matter if we did nothing but laze because there was water and cool shade and plenty of fish and lizards to eat.

The creature machines came out of the cracks in the wet. A goanna droan whirring in its servos and lazy tongue flicking out to taste the ground ahead. Its skin yeller and black pixel speckled scales with soft underbelly warmed by the rocks. Looking for metal scraps to scavenge and dead meat to pick through or anything, really, it wasn't fussy, just a gut on legs to eat whatever would keep it going till the next feed. Two hairy bigdog robos came jerking up the side of the canyon making a awful racket from their engines. They were in the hunt for new parts and they scared off the goanna droan. They would of scared me off too, but Smoov could block them with his linkmaker and they didn't come any closer. Wild bigdogs weren't fast but they would never stop till they hunted down their tucker. And then there were other creatures living in the cracks in the rocks that were older than the machines, older even than the old world, older than the words I'm using to write. Those creatures, you couldn't see them nor hear them but they were there in the gentle breeze and in the shadows of the lines in the faces of the stone though they only came out in the dark.

The Wotcher passed by overhead every night, it was a spark moving lower in the sky than the stars. When I was small I used to go running to catch it but I never could. It was too high up. It moved more slow than the other lights that tracked the sky when dark came up. It was big too, and broody, and there was a strangeness to it, like it didn't belong in the night sky. It was put there by them as who came before and it carried all their thoughts. Their dreams was stored up there if only we could listen hard enough it'd tell the secret for how to get back there. That's what Isa thought, anyway. She thought it would yield up the key for reseeding the gigacities and all the backroads crowd could rise up from the muck and live in that place where the glittering buildings grew tall and tangled together like vines. Smoov choofed his evening time smoke before a show. He always said he had to open the channels and clear the decks so he could get himself right for the Wotcher's wavy ravings which came down for the showmans with the right codes to accept the trancemission. And sure enough Smoov would pick up the Wotcher's sounds and pictures from his linkmaker as it went over and he would pass on for all in the desert backroads camps to see through his show. It was my job to keep the gear right and he taught me to write it all down so he could look later and see the patterns forming.

Smoov smoked up and looked through his notes, mumbling his ravings, happy as a bastard on father's day. He tweaked his link to the Wotcher's trancemission while me and Isa wandered the gorge like babbies. We were naked and following each other through the daze, the older creatures watching from cracks in the stone walls. It was so quiet except for the insects humming a tune that is the frequency of the whole world. The whole thing more than its separate parts, each dusty day in that coolsweet place bursting with life, fat with the babby of midday heat that grew into soft sunset viewscreen to another place. I didn't have to say nothing to Isa, we could see inside of each other, we could speak with no words. We stayed the whole season until the storm clouds stopped coming and the creek dried up and the fishes all dead and the brumby trucks showed up.

Dust cloud on the horizon first, then the growl of engines and in the distance the thumping of their sound systems. Smoov switched his linkmaker off right away but it was too late. They'd got a fix and were coming fast, sniffed out Smoov's link to the Wotcher and they wanted a piece of it. All the gear was spread far, we'd passed the whole wet there. Isa and Smoov working to pack but all I could do was stare. There were all kinds of trucks in the backroads, some were left over from the time of the gigacities and were slaved to camps and did their bidding. Some were indies, which is short for indie pendants but I dunno where their pendants are hung from anymore, maybe behind their viewscreens. The indies took their transport contracts where they could, doing work and hauling riders who would trade patches for the truckdream haze. Indies always had the best haze, it was something they made in their alkaloid truckjuice synthfacs and the trucks with the best haze found the riders with the best linkmade patches to tweak their trucking freeks and make them feel right. It was how the backroads worked. Then sometimes there were brumbies that didn't truck with no riders or contracts and went rogue. This mob of brumbies that come in to the gorge were run by a big black bastard called the Brumby King. It rained fear down on the backroads. Chrome stacks howling and ten wheels grinding and rumbling the ground as it rolled with its mob towards our camp.

Chapter 2

The brumby mob roaded in order and they kept to it tight. First came the second, the Left Tenant. It was shining white with blue trim and so proud of its painted scrollwork in western patterns. Real classic look and the other trucks in the mob followed. They each had their own colour scheme, one with candy apple green and purple and bright yeller highlights, one with crazy patterns of light blue lines on a dark blue body, one grey with thick black markings, arrow heads and barbs and geometric magic encasing wicked wheel arches and chrome trim, one with moving glyphs shifting right on top of angled lines and a snarling grill. They pranced on in gunning their engines and glowing neon running lights in the fading sun. And then at the end, the Brumby King itself powered into the gorge. It was dinged with buckled panels and stained with rust, mud and grassy tufts stuck up under the running boards. The others were vain in their looks but the Brumby King's pride was in its dusty scars. They circled around, thumping out bass beats from their sound systems that shook out the birds from the trees. The dust flowed up in clouds. Smoov had been gathering up the showgear, and then he saw me standing and he cuffed me upside the head.

'Stash the gear, dickhead' he said. The sweat soaked through his stained shirt and his eyes lit and wild.

I were frozen in fear, dazed from the slap and me mouth open slack in wonder at those brumby trucks massing and grooving to get in close to where they could take a shot at Smoov. Smoov had done plenty of chats with indie trucks but these wild brumbies chilled him same as me. They were smart as, they could do a pretty good job of fixing themselves up and even make babby trucks. Different story if they were indies, but he wasn't going to try anything on with this mob, they were powerful machines built of steel and rust and pain, and packing rounds of bullets made from bone and scraps of shrapnel from roadside wrecks and they gushed tongues of fire from their flamers. Some trucks could be tamed but not this mob run by the Brumby King, wheezing smoke out through its stacks but it wasn't no diesel, you could tell just to look.

They circled around their King and formed up about half a click from the camp. The ground shook from the hammering of their engines and the rumbling of the rocking sounds pumped from bassy woofers deep in their chassis. Smoov was almost ready to go, too busy even to clip me for still being frozen to the spot at the sight of those monsters that burned and looted everything they could find, except this time it was us there in front of them.

Isa said, 'We gotta move.'

Smoov threw a tote at me and pushed what gear he could into another bag that he hanged from me shoulder and then we were running, leaving behind what we couldn't carry. The trucks only had one road in. They couldn't get all the way around us. There was the gorge and the creek running through it on the other side, so that's where we turned while the dread sounds of a brumby jam bounced off the canyon walls with beefy bass and slack rim snare. The Left Tenant mounted the spout of a flamer on its engine cowling, tipped with the bright blue spark of pilot light, and a tongue of fire stretched out towards us. Another brumby opened up with its fifty cal, deep chattering and pinging the dust with bone bullets around us in the howling of their engines and the glowering gloom of sunset. Smoov took us up through the boulders and scree on the side of the canyon where the brumbies wouldn't pass. Though they were strong and fierce, they were leery of getting scratches on their paint and dents in their panels. Smoov pushed us on through the night, grazed hands and scratched faces in the thorny scrub as we found our way first up then down and across the creek. Then up again to the other side and away while the lights sparked out in the night from the brumby mob. They worked back and forwards on the other side searching for signs of our passing but there were none in the darkness.

A breathless strange night under the stars, creeping through the scrub as the sounds got lost in the distance and the ground we put between us and them. Smoov cursing at the lost gear but taking stock and fingering his pendant to accept the Wotcher's code. Me eyes were heavy since the rush of panic were flushed out of me body with the cold sweat drying fearstink into me clothes. I started to look back on those days spent talking with the creatures in the rocks and talking without words in that gorge in that wet season of fat rains and full billabongs bursting with life crawling up out of the cracks. Those memories stayed with me and growed inside me until I was not sure if they ever even happened. I don't know where the truth lies, which I whispered that to Isa in the cold night march while Smoov scouted ahead.

'The truth is what you can hold in your hand,' said Isa. 'The truth is the power them trucks got to raid us and murder with fitty cals and flame throwers.'

'But there's truths you can't hold. Like the truth of sunrise and sunset and the Wotcher's passing,' I said.

'Only truth that matters is what you can take away from someone else and we was droved out of the gorge by the power of them brumbies that wanted to take a piece of the Wotcher's truth from Smoov.'

'I never seen nothin like truth from Smoov's showins. It's all patterns and programs and bits that don't make no sense,' I said.

'Yair, well you're a dumbshit. I reckon the brumbies are after the Wotcher coz they're trying to crack the understanding of where they come from and what they are in the world.'

I came to see later the brumby trucks had their own truth they were chasing.

Me name is Jon Ra and I'm typing this out on an old type-writer I found one time in the dirt, it was a rotted and rustspecked case half buried in the ground. Sometimes the earth spat up stuff what'd been swallowed for a long time. The case used to be a greeny colour but it'd got all bleached and rusted. I pulled it out and later Smoov taught me the ways them different letters fit together into words and the words clumped in rows and that's how they roaded. It was an old machine, not like the seamless tech that glows inside the trucks powering themselves along the highways and the backroads. It was small enough to carry with me everywhere and though the dust got inside and made it stick, I lubed it when I could. I found a bunch of papers what I used for messages, a little stack of cards yeller with age and the ribbon could be inked with soot and sticky saps and water. I cranked them in and wrote on them, then I could shuffle them around, because sometimes it was hard to keep things straight in the order they happened. Like right now, all this stuff is all ready happened and I'm working up a start to this tale. I'm shuffling the pieces and gathering them together.

This little machine had the letters HERMES on it and I often wondered what it meaned as I sat in the flickering firelight pondering what to write. Who was that HERMES and what was her game? It were a strange name for a machine, like if I was going to name it, I'd call it Clackerplay or Writerman, something with some meaning. Instead, it was a bunch of letters with different meanings. HERMES, that's like /her/, yeah? It was a woman's /me/ only there were more than one. It's her me/s, her different forms and shapes. The different changes she made, how sometimes I could look at the light falling on Isa's face and see one thing, then when darkness came down another light might take up in her eyes. She was always shifting and changing, we all were, all the time. Writing was one way to stop the changes. When something is lettered, it's fixed on the page. You can change your story or the way you think on it, but you can't change them words. Once they've been wrote down, that's it. They're yours and you've gotta deal with it.

That was the meaning I took from it anyway. I wondered about the magic of that name, the mystery of it. There was power in the HERMES. Power everywhere you looked. There was power in the trees, in the sun, in the wind. There was power in the rolling of the wheels on the road. All you needed was an alternator and a cell to store the juice.

After I found the HERMES and Smoov taught me some lettering, it came to me in a dream a few weeks after. In the dream, I cranked words into that wording machine and it all were making sense. It wasn't quite the same machine as the one I found, this one had the same keys but it also had a power chord that I had plugged into the show cells. I finished a sentence and leaned in. I took a big whiff of it and the smell was like nothing I'd known, it nearly knocked me down, machine oil and solvents and ink and something underneath.

The smell of truth.

I knew then it was a way I could use to set out me own true self. I could be free from Smoov's moody changes and the beatings and grief he gave me, which was funny really because it was Smoov who showed me writing in the first place so I could document his shows and I kept all the trancecrypts in the typewriter case along with these pages here. Smoov showed me the shapes of the letters all lined up on a grid, and you turned the crank for a new line and the machine moved one row in the tab and together the whole thing rattled out lines of letters running down the page and across the page it spelled out words. The typewriter is an instrument to take measurements of your mind, and it leaves behind road signs on the page to show the way.

Now I still got this typewriter and no more of Smoov's trance-crypts to write down. Just how I found a way inside meself. I'm telling you this story and it's the truth. It's all true, every word of it, I swear, written in campfire smoke and truckdream haze aftertaste. Smoov showed me writing to write down the notes of his shows. He showed Isa too, but she didn't take to it like me. She was always more interested in being a showman herself and interpreting the trancemissions from the Wotcher. She reckoned the Wotcher held all the knowing of the past and if she could find the right link to get into it and extract the knowing we could rise our selves up and live in the glittering gigacities again. The machines would all work how they should and not be scavenging for bodies and parts just to live and there would be a system again, a straight system like what they'd had back then where the buildings talked to each other, grew in amongst each other like a forest and the world was a sweet and easy place.

Smoov thought it too but he was all for interpreting the signs and meanings of the Wotcher's leavings. He was looking for a pattern in the jumbled sounds and images beamed down from on high each night. But for Isa, it was different, she didn't have no time for patterns. She wanted to get straight at the heart of things and find a way to talk direct to the Wotcher and get the secrets. She went at it straight, like a goanna to a feed, to find a way into the coding of the Wotcher's trancemissions so that the desert backroads could raise itself from the dust and the troddendown mud.

She was always tweaking her link to the Wotcher and looking over Smoov's shoulder for tips and so it was up to me to find out the ways of the typewriter's lettering and keep track of Smoov's showings. Smoov was a picture showman going from camp to camp and they'd come from miles around to see what he'd do with the lightning up on the screen, which was really just a white sheet strung up between two rusting shipping cans. We'd travel on the road showing hellfire pictures for folks to know the way of things. Telling the stories of the end times and the broken down system and them trucks what came screaming along the desert highways and thrumming their tech.

Chapter 3

We fell out of the wet season and wandered the backroads shanty towns, building back up the show gear after the raid and trying to steer clear of any brumby trucks. It's all mixed up in me head. I'm shuffling the deck, trying to find a way to order things. One night we was in a camp and saw the Wotcher show coming in, it was another showman called Dane Roadson. The pictures he lit from the Wotcher shined on the screen, fragments of the old times and put together with trucksong and static fills. One stuck in me memory, a picture of a bold black truck rolling on an open highway where all the lanes were clear. It roaded fast and the rider sat up high in control. They must have had some wicked tech back then to make a truck so tame like that, I was in awe. Roadson shifted on to the telling part and started up his rambling of lessons on how to live and how to pull together and hear the Wotcher's static in our own lives and find the pattern of the knowing of the old times. The gigacities were wasted and deadly now but if the Wotcher could be tuned right, we could take them back. All the people from the camp and the lands around were there to hear it and they sat while he did his thing, but that night he was too high and by the end there weren't much meaning to be taken from it. He didn't put it all together like a good showman would. Me and Isa ate corn cobs charred with coal and chicken grease, and sat on the ground as the camp folk wandered past in the dark. Mangy dogs ranging around just out of firelight, fighting and fucking. Me bones got the jump on me smarts and I turned to Isa and tried to pash her, but she wouldn't have a bar of it, though our arms and legs were touching. We were sitting close and she didn't seem to mind that too much. Me dick was hard as. Smoov was off somewhere doing deals, swapping patches and haggling for tobacco and ganja and cactusflower grog.

'I'm not gunna,' she said.

'Aw, come on,' I said.

'Nah, I gotta keep me head. I'm gunna be showman one day too. There's more to life in this world than what you can see in the backroads, and showin's the way to get a window on the gigacities.'

'Showin's not all there is,' I said.

'It's the secret of findin out the Wotcher's knowin and the seeds of the past times and how to get back to what we've all been cut separate from,' she said.

'Ah I'm sick of hearin of the old times. Howdya know it was so good back then?' I said.

'It's in the pictures of the gigacities, in the fragments from the Wotcher's trancemission, the towers of light and the buildings that spoke to each other and the system of the world that worked so sweet,' she said.

I tried it on again, slipping me arm around her but she turned away. I said, 'Don't you see how we could be together and I could get outta here away from Smoov and his beatins?'

'I gotta stick by Smoov and learn the secrets of the show, so as I can crack the Wotcher's knowin of the gigacities. It's more than just a matter of makin enough connections in the patterns to find out the truth. Smoov's on the wrong track, and I know I still gotta lot to learn, but I reckon there's a way to get inside the Wotcher direct.'

'I don't care nothin for the Wotcher.'

'You should care. Smoov's blind in his thinkin about it, but maybe there's a clue from the Wotcher, maybe teamed up with a truckmind I could find the key and reseed a gigacity and lead the backroads folk back there.'

'Don't be so up yerself,' I said.

'Whadda you know about anythin?'

'Not much but I dunno how many more beatins from Smoov I can take. Carn, let's leave him and his stupid show. We could start our own show. He's on a bum steer anyway, like you said.'

'Smoov's shifty, but he's me dad,' she said. 'He keeps things to himself and won't let me in on all the different codes to channel the Wotcher. I need to stick it out with him a bit longer before I can form me own show.'

I wondered if she just didn't like me that much but the signs were there sometimes that she did so I kept me candle lit.

Roading, always roading. One shit heap after another. Traffic on the highway clogged with people and trucks and trolleys and droans skating over cracked tarmac and humming in the air. Flapples flying high up in the sky, black and rust specked shapes catching the light on bare silver claws and sharp metal beaks. They rode the air hot up off the baking ground, looking for machine meat to eat in the bodies of trucks and robo droans fallen by the way. We came up on a group of indie trucks daisy-chaining in a circle, and there wasn't nothing that could stop Smoov from going down there and working a chat with them. Indies were a different matter to brumbies. They still played by the code of the road and could be wrangled with patches to give up their truckdream haze that they made in onboard synthfacs. Smoov was born with the gift of the gab and he loved the taste of haze so he pulled out his linkmaker. It was a scratched up slab of aluminium that you held in your and and it tuned your mind in to the trucks' frequency, something from outta the past that only the showmans and a few others like truck detailers had control of. Me and Isa stood by the gear while he blinked the patchfile tags through his linkmaker on the trucks' freek. Down off the side of the road, in a small gully, they grouped in the groove, pumping a rocking dub through their sound systems. It was a growing, growling mess, heavy bass and drumthump hitting you in the chest so you felt it rather than heard it. Felt the power of it, felt the falling snare hit rimshot crack on the frontbeat and the lazybones shaker on the back. Horns dripping wet with delay and the whole thing was a jammy vibe right from the start. They were patterned indies, dressed in decals and lightshifting scrollwork moving all the time, you couldn't look at them for long because you wouldn't move at all, you'd just be there in a trance.

Smoov was well skilled and used to the ways of indie trucks. He knew how to wrangle them, how to tame them with patches, make them do what he wanted done. I'd watched him do it and I learned a few things over the years. I'd learned how the trucks would trade with riders and showmans like Smoov, how they'd swap their truckdream haze for patches that the riders made to trip out their truckminds. And the sounds they jammed shifted and changed over the years in different phases too, rolling through their culture like the phases of the moon meeting back around the beginning again. This time Smoov was trying to get rid of some old junk patches and at the same time to feel his way into this new mob. They might have some contacts, there might be some roading. They could help us shorten the time between two points in the backroads, or give him some sweet haze that he could get high off.

He went down to the mob and they didn't move or nothing. There were droans skittering and flapples flying around, scrounging for parts, but this wasn't a big meet up and there were slim pickings. The indies didn't give any sign they'd seen Smoov, they didn't care. He was just a puny bloke and they were humming with power and tech and gleaming with moving glyphs and paintwork. Beats rocking, donks throbbing, swapping sounds and patchtag files to change the patterning of their minds, and Smoov always had something tasty, something good to share and trade for the haze that kept the backroads running nice and smooth like the outside of Smoov's linkmaker worn shiny from being clutched in his hand.

Down by the side of the creek I sat with Isa while we waited and she told me the story of the creatures in the rocks that came out at night when no one's looking and stole the breath from young babbies and how the indie trucks came on the land and rutted like wild animals, smashing into each other and flying sparks in the night sky and making babby trucks that over time had come to learn how to make the haze to pull the best riders with the best patches.

I sat there letting the sound of her voice fall around me like soft rain. I was in heaven. Then she started talking about this bloke called Crow and I snapped out of me dream, remembering that crow on Mum's body.

'Crow wears a coat made from shredded truck tyres and he's a scavenger, a trickster. He roads slow from camp to camp, stickin his beak in to any business where there's profit to be made from the shreds of others' pain. He's always ready to extract his toll from sufferin. But he's got a magic about his self, he can change his shapes dependin on the company he keeps and he knows the ways of the backroads truckriders and how to live off the land as well. He can turn others' minds around to do his own work with a crinkle of his white eye.'

I said, 'I never heard that before.'

'It's true,' Isa said. 'True fact. I ain't seen him meself but I seen the marks he's made in the world.'

Later on Smoov came back and he was high on wild indie truckdream haze. He talked a hundred mile an hour about them indies that was also tuning to the Wotcher's freek.

He said, 'One thing to do is to play to a indie's pride. They're all vain and they like to have things no other truck has got. If you can offer them something rare, they'll trade with you for it. Trade for roadin or truckdream haze. You gotta be careful coz you never know what they is gunna do, but if you can find the right truck, you can make a team, truck and rider. You can make a pair, like a pair between a showman and the Wotcher. Hook them through the link and show them you got patches to trade. You can even use the patches to get the trucks to do what you want sometimes, it hits them like haze hits a human. And like haze, it's a leash you can jerk.'

Smoov ranted on and on though we had heard it many times before. But there was always something you couldn't predict with Smoov, always some surprise coming out of his mouth. That night he said this: 'Them trucks is gettin more and more interested in the ways of interpretin the Wotcher's trancemissions. They don't got the same kind of thinkin as a human, but they know the Wotcher's part of their own past too. I reckon they got a feelin of kinship with the Wotcher, like sometime back they come from the Wotcher and the Wotcher's got the keys to their codin, see, and if they knowed what it was, they could take control of the present and breed their own hybrids. They're loadin fragments from the Wotcher's frequency into their trucksongs and puttin them together like a showman would, to find the patterns.'

I could see Isa was hooked up intense in Smoov's words, she was listening hard. What I took from what he said was the trucks thought they could find their own past in the Wotcher and use it to make a better future, like we were trying to do. Then the haze took Smoov over and he turned mean and swiped me with his fist till the sparks flew in me head. And looking back, maybe I should have done things different, taken me swag and headed out on me own right there and then. But maybe it doesn't make any difference.

Next day we saw a camp of desert people. They'd been there long before the flapples and bigdogs and trucks and goanna droans came, and they'd be there longtime still. They knew the places to dig for water, they knew the ways of hunting meat, they knew how to cook and how to live off that land. They didn't want nothing to do with the indie trucks what roared and shook the rutted roads and they didn't want nothing to do with dusty riders and showmans and sandblasted followers of truckdream haze. And I thought they'd got the right idea and we got the wrong of it.

Chapter 4

It was later on. The moon had fatted and wasted with none to account and no more sign of brumbies. We were on the plainlands and down in the dirt, digging for old hardware in the rubble of broken ruins. Me and Isa picked through the muck, mining for data on dead media drives. Smoov was a little way off, wild scraggyface hair but digging carefully. He could scan the drive to pull the fragments of pictures or sounds and splice them in to spice the show from the Wotcher. He was a showman, and the showmans were the only ones who could extract the data and interpret what came up from those wells beneath the earth and from the shining Wotcher up above.

Isa's brown hands were working next to mine, going over broken cases and copper wires. I looked up and caught her eyes and she smiled. I lived for those smiles. They were me campfire embers on a cold desert night. Smoov collected a clatter of junk up over the rise. Always digging, looking for the pieces that were going to make the puzzle fit together. But there wasn't no fit, no together, just the pieces. I knew it by then, even if I was too young and dumb to say anything. There was only the puzzle, only the smooth surface, nothing underneath. Especially nothing in the junk we dug up out of the ground, just bits and bites of random signs left behind from people who were long gone from the earth.

I climbed over a mound and reached down to pull up a hefty case, to find underneath was a creature that looked like a snake with dirty metal skin lying there against the ground. It was so still I didn't see what it was until I was right up close. I siezed up. It glistened wet and nasty, ten hands long and thick like a root. Its tongue flicked. Its skin was black holes in the world. Its red eye glowed in the shadows and it made a shivering slivering whisper as it reared up on its back and looked right at me. I called out, me voice quivering.

'Smoov... There's some kind of snake.'

Smoov looked up but he was slow in moving. Isa's eyes flashed on the snake. She came closer to take a look.

'Stay back,' I said.

She wouldn't. She wanted to see and she wanted to get close to it, her eyes bright and burning to see the knowing of the new creature. She took another step forwards and bent down, reaching out her hand, the snake struck and bit her wrist. She cried out and that's when Smoov came rushing over. The snake slivered off into the garbage. Smoov turned on me, eyes red and ruddy beard scraggling with rage.

'What've you done, you fucken idjit? You stirred it up, didinya?'

He pushed me rough out of the way, trying to get to Isa.

'No I didn't it wasn't like that,' I said.

Sickening real fast, Isa paled and fell to the ground. She cried and whimpered.

He gathered her up in his arms and took her rushing back to where we were camped, next to an old and rusted truck cab on its axles, its windows hung with tarps. Smoov ripped off a piece of cloth from his shirt and tied up her arm real tight. Laid her on the ground and said, 'Don't move, there there.' Busted up a couple of sticks on his knee and tied them to her arm so she couldn't move it.

I watched him from behind. I didn't want to get in the way but I wanted to see what I could do to help.

The skin on her arm started to turn blue and scale up like the dirty metal scales from the snake thing, hard and cold. She was going into shock, sweating and shivering. The poison was spreading. She started to moan. Sunlight glinted off the sweat on her skin. I leaned in to touch her.

'Git away,' Smoov yelled.

He swung the back of his hand and clipped me on the head. Like it was my fault Isa got bitten. I went down to the edge of the ruins and cried where the robos and the crows pecked over bones and circuit boards and I hoped Isa would be OK.

*

I kept me eyes out for the snake but it was long gone. Isa snake-bitten and no telling what would happen to her.

Smoov glowering.

'Fucken idjit,' he said.

'Fair go, Smoov. It wasn't my fault,' I said.

'Bullshit it weren't. You stirred it up, you unco bludger. Everything you ever done turns to shit in yer hands.'

'Na, it wasn't like that, Smoov.'

But there wasn't no telling him. He was itching for a blue. He raised up his right hand to hit me. I shied away from it till the next thing he was swinging a big round blow with his left what caught me in the head.

I put me hands up too late. The right came back around straight after, me head exploding from the shock and I lost me feet. I was on the ground with a screwed up face, hands clutching at the air, trying to get him off. He dropped the dead weight of his knees in me chest and puffed the wind out of me and those fists kept coming, arcing around like rocks on the ends of the chains of his arms. Three four five times, each one booming in me ears, louder than trucksong, lightning sheets of pain with each shock sending off red and black and blue colours in behind me tight closed eyes.

He took his fill of me like he was drinking a draught, and when the anger left him he lifted up his knee and took to his feet. I laid on the ground. The blood flowed first then the tears came with the ache.

'Yer a fucken waste of space,' Smoov mumbled under his breath. He took off back to where Isa laid.

It was over in just one or two minutes but the pain stayed and leaked into me bones and me dreams at night.

Isa spent a fevered night that sweated and cried like the night I lost me Mum. I cried for Isa and for me poor busted face. Isa called out in a snakedream. Smoov kept her real still to give her a chance to fight the poison instead of it hitting her all at once. When the light came on in the morning we packed the gear and roaded to where Smoov knowed of some healing folks on the track to Hind Pass where we was headed for the next showing.

Got to their camp rideless come sundown. The healing folks sat round their campfire. Bald white fella in a rooskin coat and his missus with pierced ears, lobes long and hanging down to her shoulders. Smoov told them what happened and they brung out their bags and their herbs and smoking incense.

Isa let them look at her arm and they checked her pulse and eyes and her tongue, bloke fussing over his tote bag and the missus looking on steady.

Missus said, 'Them slinky snakes has been eatin of the poison ground of the past and so theys be come poison themself.'

The bloke said, 'Nah, the slinky snakes *is* the poison. They've come up outta the ground wrung by the poison of the old times. Before the glitterin gigacities falled into rubble, there were no snakes. Then the viris ate out the guts of the machines of the past and brung the smashed-up trash and snowfallen ashes. Now the slinky snakes is been birthed.'

'Ah, youse don't know nothin bout the past,' said Smoov. 'It's all just dodgy guessin and imaginins. Now tell me, what can yer do for her?'

'No tellin. I seen only three others who been bit, so it's hard to say. Two fellas died right there and one scaled up and become metal till he were ate by a flapple.'

Isa turnt her eyes on them weakly and said, 'I'm all right. If I was gunna cark it, it would of happened before now. I'm not gunna be ate by a flapple neither.'

She scratched at the metal scales on her arm.

'It's true,' said the bloke. 'She's crook all right but I don't think she's gunna die. The poison been slowed long enough now for her system to soak it up.'

Smoov grunted then said, 'Boy, get down the creek and fetch some water for our friends.'

I did what he said. We couldn't stay there though, we had to get moving. There was always danger from brumby trucks and so when Isa's fever broke enough and the sun was high up in the sky we set off for Hind Pass, Isa slung over Smoov's shoulder. I carried all the gear plus weedseed damper and honeybee nectar and tea and tobacco. Smoov with his ganja and cactusflower grog brewed in plastic bottles. All that was left of the old world was plastic. The grass grew high up roadside in front of mountains of plastic bottles, plastic bags, plastic buckets, plastic shapes, all that plastic greyed out and sometimes the earth throwed it up, it didn't have no colour no more, it was grey as dust. When the ground vomits it up, there's people in rags picking through the trash of old time. People with bags full of rope and copper wire and fallen ash on top of the ash, stinking oily tides of trash washed up from the dirty land. Cliffs fallen down, tongues of fire, tongues of land licking tongues of black water eating up the ground.

Isa was weak and shivering, there was a nervous feeling in me belly as I remembered how close she'd got to the slinky snake and I thought maybe she wanted to get bit. I didn't know what it meant but I was putting it together with her thoughts and reckonings on how she wanted to team with a truckmind to crack the Wotcher and that she'd need Smoov's linkmaker to do that, and maybe from the poisoned ground of the poisoned machines, the slinky snakes had brought a new change into the scene. And what chances Isa might be willing to take to get around Smoov's blocking and stalling and find out the knowing of the system that ran the gigacities. Smoov was still giving me the cold shoulder silent treatment like it was all me fault and me face was broken and throbbing from the beating. There was rain on that track through the backroads to Hind Pass.

A rumble in me guts and a rig rolling on the road. It was a silver Kenworth and it was covered in glittering glyphs and symbols, made me broken heart race to see it and feel its rumble and hear its throaty roar as it came closer. Smoov cursed and tried to hail it on his wavy linkfinder but he was lumbered with Isa and before he could dial in the right freek it was too late, the Kenworth was dust.

So on we trudged through that day and the next and before noon on the third I saw something was dogging our tail, I could see the dust behind. We kept on going, fast as we could, which wasn't that fast. Pretty soon it was clear that the follower wasn't moving any faster neither, though it was gaining slowly.

'Is it brumby trucks?' I asked.

Smoov glowered. 'They would of took us before now if it were trucks. It's somethin else.'

'Let's pull over and hide in the scrub while they go past,' said Isa.

'We got no idea what it could be back there, nor what is their program. We keep movin till Hind Pass,' said Smoov.

We kept on that road under the blare of the white sun and the hot breath of the air sucking water out of our skins with its dry kiss. A riot of white clouds high up in the gasping sky. Smoov looked back to take a measurement, the chrono and the tachyo cranking in his linkmaker, figuring time and speed and distance.

Isa was pale and scared. Being snakebitten changed her. The skin round her arm was all scaled up with mealy metal flakes.

'It's bad, whatever's followin. I can feel it,' she said.

Smoov didn't say nothing, but I could tell he were afraid. Afraid for Isa and afraid of the follower. I caught the vibe off of Smoov and his showman's instincts so I pushed us along a little faster. If we could stay ahead of them till sundown we could lose them in the dark.

'How come they're goin so slow?' I said.

'How come you're goin so slow? Keep moven yer arse,' Smoov said.

So we kept on all through that smokey afternoon, the slow race a grindstone around our necks, playing on our minds.

'We should just stop and face em, see whatever's comin,' I said.

'Whaddaya know of it anyway? Just keep movin. When night comes we're gunna get off the road.'

The afternoon stretched and time wasn't fixed but flowing thick like engine oil in axle grease. I gritted me teeth and put me back into the haul, and the sun slowed as it tracked across the sky. Off in the distance to the east the green scrub drab on red wiggly mountains. In the west the sun a burning eye hole sinking at last beneath the line of the earth and the follower at the selfsame distance behind, judging by the dust and the view we could get of their movements from the linkmaker.

Dark fell quick and we didn't waste no time getting off the road a short way and then Smoov messed up our tracks with bags and found a hollow place in the ground to stow the show gear and we crept off back up the road never hoping to see whatever it was that was following. Rustling in the spinifex spooked me but it was just nightime creatures and off in the distance robo bigdogs whining on the hunt. We found a place to lie real quiet and the night stretched longer than the day before but we were tired. We found some sleep inbetween fitful turnings of eyes scanning the blue black horizon for signs of any moving thing.

In the morning we went back and all the show gear had been found and looted. It could of been by a flapple or an animal or robo but there was only one thing taken, a pendant of Smoov's that gave him the codes to the Wotcher's trancemission to use in his linkmaker. He went dark and cursed the sky.

'What was it that got taken, Dad?' Isa said.

'It was a pendant, that's all. A link to the past. It's only just a memento. It's got no use, and no use to the one who took it neither. I remember all the glyphs and codes in me head. Carn, we got some ground to cover today to make it to Hind Pass by sundown.'

Smoov tried to play cool about the pendant but I could tell its loss hurt him. Isa warmed herself by the fire and said, 'I wonder if what was followin us could of been Crow.'

'Ain't no Crow, it's all bullshit. Keep yer drongo imaginins for yer show preps,' said Smoov.

'It's true as I heard it,' Isa said. And after a bit she said, 'Can I look through the show notes for patterns?'

'Nope. They're only for showmans' eyes.'

'But Jon's no showman.'

'That's right. He's a ugly dumbshit halfwit that keeps all the gear right and does what he's told.'

I dunno why I didn't run from them both except for the times I could see Isa's smile. I boiled up the billy and we had some tea and roady made from weedseed flour, water and honeybee nectar. Smoov smoked up like he always did and off we roaded, this time with nothing following behind but empty space and Smoov got stoned and brooded on the pendant that was stolen and I wondered if it was Crow that had been the follower and that rifled the gear and stole the pendant, like Isa said. And in the sky a flapple rode the air moving off the salt pan now the sun was up. The blasted landscape all around was so lonely and wrecked but still sometimes I had to stop myself from getting caught up in it. One minute you cursed its white emptyness and then the next you rounded a corner and saw a new view of wonder and beauty.

We made it through that next long day, Isa weaker and sick still, like she had seen a ghost. Maybe that's what passed us in the night, I don't know, or maybe it was just being snakebit, but I thought I saw a glimpse of Smoov's pendant when she moved her hand from pocket to pack. I kept me mouth shut and put one foot in front of the next all the way to Hind Pass, about twelve clicks south and then we could see the shape of its tin walls in the red desert and it was a happy sight.

Chapter 5

We hit Hind Pass shanty town with the show gear all stashed. Isa weak still but she flashed me a smile, friendly face in the frowns and tears of the road. Smoov was grim of look, he was starting to get right for fixing on the Wotcher and the trancemission he would channel. He was roadwise and able, always thinking on the next move, but it was up to me to scan the faces to see how things were going to go down in the camp. The folks were gathering for the show, getting ready to hear what they could take from Smoov's pictures and the messages he brought down from the Wotcher. They saw the show as a way of coming together and trying to understand how the pieces all fit. And Smoov sold them on the idea that one day if they listened hard enough and gathered enough connections through the patterns of the Wotcher's signal there'd be a message that would shine down and put back the system from the past time.

Kids ran past the show cart shouting, 'Show, show, show,' and Smoov still with that steely look in his eyes. One kid ran alongside us hitting a old tyre with a stick. The sun set through the ash in the air. It was a smaller following than I thought we would get. We'd been there before, it's on the show circuit from camp to camp through the desert backroads. Dogs were lying on the ground and chooks clucking and pecking and the air rasped me throat with dust and town smell.

The kids following us along besides the cart scratched at the tarp and tried to see what was under the covers. Smoov smacked their hands away. One kid looked at Smoov, dirty face tangle of hair.

'Is the Wotcher gunna come down and save us against the brumbies?' the kid said.

'Wotcher don't come,' Smoov said. 'Wotcher passes by high in the sky.'

'But the horse head prophet said—'

'Wotcher don't make no innerference. It just tells its messages and the showmans interprets them so you know how to live. Maybe there'll be a message from the Wotcher in the show for you tonight.'

We roaded in on a track lined with shacks. Women sat on mats woven from plastic mined from the wreckage of the past and what came after. Blokes were smashed off their face on cactusflower grog brewed in plastic bags buried in the ground. Kids running around everywhere, and everywhere I looked I saw the faces of the starving and the empty. Smell of sour sweat and cookfire smoke, drying rabbit skins, chillies on strings.

Smell of blood and guts fresh from butcher knives, smell of sewer and rotted garbage, smell of meaty smokehouse. Smell of diesel jenny, smell of newmade molecules from truckjuice alkaloid synthfac.

We rolled up to the show place, all laid out in the centre of camp. Many times before we had done the show. It was our meat and our bed, it was Smoov's lifework, sweat of his yakka. It was his raising and his following and it would be his dying too, and the ending of his road was coming up fast. He rolled up a smoke and sat in the shade of the cart while he readied his linkmaker for the Wotcher's pass. In behind his eyes the trancemissions came every night for him to choose from and pattern the Wotcher's message.

The kids gathered round now, and the old folks came too. I'd been charging the cells all day, charging them off the alternator sucking juice from the friction of the rolling wheels of the cart and the turn of windprop. I creaked a case off the cart and started stowing the gear. Smoov puffed on his smoke, blowing great grey gouts of it from his nose. He was getting ready for his role. Isa sat by the crates I took out. She studied Smoov, studied his face and his hands, making sure she took in all the things she could. She was prepping to innerface with the Wotcher's trancemission herself. There's a secret way to it, a secret that only the showmans like Smoov knew — how to find the right freeks. They kept it to themselves through secret rites and the secret language and the linkmakers the showmans past on through the ages to catch the Wotcher's message.

Sun went down, lightning in the west crackling dry sheets. No smell of rain. I strung the white tarp from where the show would come forth. And then the Wotcher spun, moving slow and the flash of it came up from the east like a shining eye in the sky. There was a gasp from the folks in the camp as it passed and the wonderment from the crowd that something like that could be so high up and move so slow and regular, and the power of those who must have put it there, and the hope that there'd be another way back to the time when a vessel could be launched and floated like a star. In the wake of its passing it left its messages in the showman's linkmaker and out of the crackle of static and noise came the signs the showmans used to earn their meat and their smoke. They could listen the Wotcher. They could sing the signal and tune to the freek of it.

The kids were quiet as it passed but after it was gone they started chattering, even the older ones who I'd seen come many times were excited for the show, that crackling message from on high. Wotcher gave the knowing that something better had come before and maybe one day someone would piece it all together where it all made sense and we would find the road back into the gigacities. The earth would be calm green again and the waters blue like in the Wotcher picture shows and the buildings of the gigacities would grow in the ground like concrete trees with steel leaves and they would talk together like they used to and suckle the poison from the ground.

Darkness gathered and the crowd gathered thicker too. They were tanked up and ready for the show, jostling and straining for a better view of the screen. Smoov knowed how to play it. He let it build and build until the right moment and then he motioned me and I hit the light and the screen lit bright white and then circles of colour swirled and swirled with the shadows of the insects humming in the air. Smoov came forwards from out of the gloom, head downcast and full of the Wotcher's trancemission. The gabbling crowd went silent. Isa sat behind soaking it all up, seeing how Smoov did it. He flowed his jacket behind him and sat down at the decks and slotted one of the dead drives we harvested, using a slaved truckmind saved from the muck to randomise the pictures like trucks did with wavey trucksounds, mixing traces and trances, the light spreading out in waves from the screen until we could see a bloke's face forming in the patterns. The Rider. A face hard and worn. He was riding up a rig painted blue, the Blue Mule that belched black smoke from its chrome smoke stacks and high up in the rider's cab he sat, so tight with that rig you wouldn't know there was a space between them. The brown desert landscape flowed past. This was a well known clip but then there was a jump and a new piece of picture formed up on the screen. You could sense the feelings of the crowd as they hushed even further and were sucked in to the new piece of the puzzle. The

Rider was out of the cab and chained up and he was beaten by blokes with sticks and then the new part of the trancemission finished in a funnel of snow and dust and specks caught in a beam of light. Smoov remixed the clip, looping it back in with other splices, cuts dug deep from the ground, but the folks was there to see the latest Wotcher clip. Sometimes the new ones fit with what had come before, working up a whole picture of the Blue Mule show beamed down from on high and mixed with truck rumbling sound and static snow to trip the heads of the camp folk.

Smoov played the decks, swirling pixelfire ash from the crying sky until there were only the images from the Wotcher burning into everyone's eyes, and into their hearts as well. That big Blue Mule gunned itself over rises and through the highways of the world with its Rider in tune. Though the Rider didn't have no linkmaker, he didn't need one because them who had come before could channel their rigs without even a freek, just the power of their thoughts. The folks were watching, mouths open and silent in front of the screen. Truckdream haze and cactusflower grog worked through their systems and jacked their eyes and ears to the view from the time when all the gigacities worked and the world's machines were neat and orderly on the slavegrid with no droans nor brumbies roaming the lands. Smoov cranked up the pace, bringing the sounds and pictures up loud and letting them drop away again before the big finish. The camp folks were there with him, they started to get to their feet and move in time with the sounds, swaying with the rhythm of the dancing pictures. Right at the peak of it in the smoke from the fires and the dust risin from the stamping of the feet, the madness came to take hold and Smoov took up the mike. He started his chanting rant.

'Camps folk and show followers, I'm callin, I'm tellin so youse can hear the message of the Wotcher that passes by and the pictures I'm gunna put together for you to see different ways of bein and new changes comin down the pipeline from on high.'

The crowd swelled, calling back into the starry night, dusty moon shining through moths flying round the lamp of the picture beam. The words rose up from the people: 'Tell it.'

Now it were my turn to roll. I cranked a sheet into the typewriter and started to follow Smoov's flow. I couldn't get it all down, of course I couldn't, but I did me best to catch it as Smoov went on. I saved all the sheets neatly in the typewriter case so Smoov could look back on his telling later and puzzle over the meaning of it.

'When the Wotcher passes and beams its message, it's tryin to show what the past was like from the other side of the screen. It's dark when the Wotcher passes into darkness and it's dark up there in the high of the sky. So we can't see in the clear light of the screen, we've only got pieces of it. We're puttin the pieces together to make a whole picture. But we gotta be patient and wait for the right time. Like the Rider who's gettin beaten in this new scene, we gotta be tough and cop that beatin, we gotta keep our beliefs intact and whole in these times. It's always darkest right before the sun rises. We're gunna get back to where things come easy and everythin could be dug up from the ground and floated on the air, before all the changes started and brought the gigacities down, before there was bigdog robos and droans and flapples. There's a pure time, a real time, and the Wotcher's got the way of it if youse've got the steadiness and the insight to listen it and see it. If youse is faifull to the Wotcher's messages, an if youse can bear the witness of its showin, youse can find a way through the backroads deserts to the time before when things worked right like they should an there weren't no poison in the groun. I ain't gunna lie. I can't promise youse it'll be easy. I can't promise a Wotcher what can come on down to the groun in the dirt of the backroads to lift youse all up to its own size. But if youse've got the ticker to grind it out and do things right with each other, the Wotcher's gunna show how to be free from the fears of flapple an bigdog an brumby droan.'

He hit the heights as the campfires burned up and the smoke choked and sounds swirled and the flickering images flashed in the frenzy of the moving of the bodies of the people and I saw Isa, her eyes shining in the light and she gave me a smile and I tried to take her hand but she walked off into the smoke, leaving me to stash the show gear.

*

I came out of the dream of the show, that mist of faces streaming, crying eyes, broken teeth, red cheeks, smoke ringing the lights, moths and insects flying around. All of a sudden I didn't feel right, like the people there didn't wish us well. The faces in the camp firelight and bright showstream, the press of all those bodies and all their thoughts was weighing on me, and thoughts have presence, they have weight. I looked for Isa, she was gone. Smoov'd got five or six blokes around him giving him the backslap, telling him it was a awesome show, he was the best showman around, but then there were others on the margins with sly smiles and whispers behind hands and glances that Smoov never seen.

I stumbled out of there, looking for Isa. I couldn't find her nowhere. I searched through those faces, some friendly, some hating, most just empty and caught in their own thoughts, not even noticing what was going on around or trying not to see. I walked through the camp, crooked dusty track and pathway laid out with no thought or plan, tangled rope and tin and tarp. Blokes and women sitting on stumps and sitting on the ground outside shacks and shanties, tarps and tents, humpy and lean to. All the chooks were either roosted or roasted on sticks but there were dogs, bright eyes shining in the edges of the light. Brawling and crawling, smoking and drinking and the rush of haze from truckjuice alkaloid synthfac. There were babbies crying and kids mucking around and kids sitting quiet. There was singing in one place, open throat bawling, someone laughing someone crying, weeping and shouting in the dusky dark. No centre to it, it was all edge, ends folded in on themselves, a meeting of fire and smoke, light and shadow, and all the demons of the earth and sky were come there that night, to act out their tortured shows.

Then in a flash through flapping canvas I saw Isa, she was with another bloke. They were making out. I turned and I ran. What'd I seen?

Through me tears I took corners through the camp, tripping over rope, stumbling over myself. It was dark and I came to the outside fence where the action thinned out, it was quieter, I heard the rustling of a big lizard and the whoosh swoosh of nightbird wing. I cried and shook, trying to process, but I didn't have no teraflop donk like a truckmind, just a rotten meatbrain rushing with feelings I didn't understànd nor want to know.

'It's all right. It's all right.'

It was a bloke came up out of the dark.

'If she's gone I mays well be dead,' I said.

'There's no need for cryin, thers no need for dyin. I can give yer somethin for yer ails,' he said.

'I don't think so I don't think there's nothin for this,' I said.

'That's not true. Take a little snifter of this brew.'

He held out a flask. I was so sad, I just took it from him and necked it. It burned a river of fire in me throat, it set me eyes a light and me head was scrubbed clean with a wire brush. Me thoughts were suddenly clear and I felt alive and shining.

'That's a good brew,' I said.

He laughed.

'Yeah, it's made from truckdream haze and cactusflower. Now listen,' he said, 'if it's a woman yer after, I can help. I can sing em.'

I looked at him. He were old, maybe forty maybe less, thinning hairs on his head, small white eyes too far apart, he stared, blinkless. He wore an old black coat that sucked up the gloomering firelight. He looked to me like there was roos loose in the top paddock.

'You don't look like you've had too much luck with women yerself,' I said.

'Looks is deceivin. Underneath the face, theres the skin and the bone, the cock and balls. That's where the juice comes from, mate. Now, what's yer problem?'

'I can't tell ya.'

'Lemme guess, there's someone you want that don't want you, is that it?'

'Yeah.'

'Lissen, I know you is with that showman. I'm guessin it's his daughter you've got the hots for.'

That was a shock to hear it said, but Smoov's show was well known in the backroads. This bloke could put the pieces together.

He said, 'I seen her with that other bloke just now, meself. So I'm puttin two by two. You're a young bloke, I'm sure you're well hung and fulla cum. You just want somethin to ease the chill of the night, somethin to put out the fire that's took hold of yer brain—'

'Orright, you got me number,' I said. 'There's fuck all I can do about it.'

'You know one way that this could pan out, me old digger,' he said, 'is if Smoov was not around. If Smoov was out of the picture. Then she would be showman. That's what she wants, you can tell just by lookin.'

'Mate I don't think it's so simple.'

'Oh it's simple all right. Nothin could be simpler. That showman's standin in yer way, he's houndin every day, keepin you in yer place, and her too, not lettin her know the secrets of the show, the secret rites of the showmans that they incantate under the lights, what is her birth right. I'll tell you what to do. I'll give you the word and things'll work out for you with the girl. You never will be free till that showman's gone.'

He dropped some thing in the dirt and winked at me as he turned to go. The light caught on his coat and I saw that it was made all of shredded trucktyre. I bent and picked up the thing he dropped and walked me way back through the faces to the showing place and all the time I had the knowing growing that it was Crow I'd just been talking to and I was thumbing a razored shiv that I'd picked up from the ground. Back in camp and Smoov was snoring his fucken head off. His white neck where the pulse beats was showing naked and soft in the soft firelight and me mind so full of sadness and anger. I thought I'd just let a bit of the blood out from him to see what would happen but I couldn't do it.

Chapter 6

Next day dawned slow and lonely like the churn of a river's mud. Me head was swollen from Crow's brew and me eyes caked shut. I rubbed them out and looked around and saw through the dust to the truth of things, how the pieces had fallen. Isa was with anotha bloke, and I was so caught up in me thoughts I couldn't see past me own mumbling dumbness. It played on me mind as I set the breakfast cookfire burning, heating lard in the pan, saltpig sizzling with snake egg and weedseed damper. Boiling sandy sinkhole water and stale coffee beans ground with pestle and stone for the billy. Isa was late to rise out of the swag. I didn't know what time she'd got in. She wasn't there when I'd laid down. I looked in her eyes but she didn't look back. Smoov was snoring, always the way after he'd done a show. It was another day and work to be done, hooking up the cells to the camp jenny, making things right with the show gear. And then there was the thick edge of the shiv that I kept fingering in me tote, the shiv that Crow gave me and the words he seeded that I could be free of Smoov. What was that strange Crow creature? He disappeared away like in a dream and like in a dream it hit me that it wouldn't be the last time I saw him.

Isa scratched her scaled up arm. She moved more slowly now, the poison from the snakebite had passed out of her system, though the scales spread. She squatted to eat and when she was done noshing she scrubbed the dishes clean in the sand. Coming back, she tried to sneak a look at the notes in me typewriter case. Smoov woke up right then, grumbling and mumbling to himself, and he saw what was going on right away.

'No you don't, them notes are for me only.'

'Why can't I see them?'

'One day when you're showman you can, but not yet. There's truths in there you can't understand.'

'What are you so afraid of?' she said.

'I'm not afraid of anything, but those notes are me history and they are me future as well and no one gets to look at them till I say.'

'You trust Jon with em.'

'He's not the full quid. He's never gunna show nor ride the roads. He just letters the trancecrypts.'

'Ah, I'm sick of your bullshit secrets. I'm gunna head out into camp, see if I can trade somethin for this disc drive from Lossiters Reef.'

She went off and I didn't say nothing. I gave Smoov his brekky and boiled another billy. When I stood up, I knocked his brew over. His eye slits were hard and saltpig lard shiny on his gingy beard, mad as a cut snake.

'Come ere, you dickhead.'

I cringed away from his hand but right then a bloke came up through the camp to speak to Smoov. I made myself busy with packing and the cleaning, but kept an ear on them.

The bloke wore leathers and pouches and he had on proper boots. He said, 'There's talk of trucks raidin in the backroads. A brumby mob rainin havoc down. Things are pullin apart in the camp, folks is settin out on their own. They're scared we can't protect em. And there's this new idea about the Wotcher that is a saver instead of a sayer.'

'I've been hearin the wordin on the Wotcher for a long time. There's raidin mobs out there, mate I seen em meself. Them brumbies has been after me for me link before and doubtless will again. There's nothin I can do for youse in this camp. I just road from place to place, earnin me meat and smoke and interpertin the Wotcher's signs,' said Smoov.

'Don't be coy, Smoov Ra. You got sway with yer shows. And there's more to interpreting trancemissions than gettin stoned and playing pictures.'

'I don't see what I can do,' said Smoov

'You're one of the blokes who's got an in with the camps. You got the ears of some of them who makes the calls. If you could work some politics into yer tells, the camps would be able to make a go of it, pullin together and actin as one against the brumbies.'

'I don't got no say on what I'm telled by the Wotcher,' said Smoov.

'Waddya know of the Wotcher's program, but? What's the Wotcher doin sendin messages down to earth?'

'Wotcher's gunna give us the secrets of the old time, give us secrets of the tech times and the runnin of them gigacity machines.'

'Folks wanna be saved right now. There's brumbies massin. The people is not gunna stick round if the Wotcher can't give some help against the brumby trucks. Just think on it Smoov. Just think on what yer showin and think on what's best for the camps to be seein.'

'I never do and I won't start. I don't have no say on the trancemission. I'm not beholden to any camp boy, neither. I run me own show.'

The bloke got dark then.

'Well, Smoov, there's other showmans. There's other tellers who can see what's best for the camps is best for them. There's brumby forces gatherin, and a mood for changin.'

The bloke wasn't gunna get much farther with Smoov. Smoov were proud. He'd been threatened before. It was always a dicey game being a showman. You had to keep lots of different things in your head at once and you had to be true to what came in the trancemission and in the world as you saw it on the ground in front of your eyes, too.

Isa came back then and we were ready to start getting the

show set for another night, but she was away somewhere else inside her head. Maybe her thoughts were with the show, maybe the other bloke. We came around the camps often enough, I knew I weren't the only one. What were playing on me own thoughts was another thing but then she saw me looking and she smiled and I felt the lock of her eyes and the thrill of the connection we had, no matter if there were another bloke. I was a fool and I almost threw away that shiv that the old bloke gave me, but I kept it in me tote and the words he said all tied up tight in me head.

There were plenty of talk in the camp that day of brumbies gathering in the east and later on when it was all quiet while the storm front brewed up before showtime, me and Isa went out on top of a rocky cliff to see. Clouds stacked high on top of each other up in the sky out west. All was ready with the gear, the darkness gloaming closer as we crept out of camp around the cliftop to spend some time while Smoov was making his moves and doing politics with the camp folk. Down on the plain just below we could see a mob of brumby trucks was daisychaining in the lee of the hill, windswept scrub not quite hiding them and nothing could hide the sound of that roar they made, the beating of their soundsystems louder than me heart in booming in me ears as I watched.

'What's goin on?' I said.

'They're truckruttin. I've heard the stories, but this is the first time I've seen em doin it.'

She came closer to me, the warmth of her body next to mine. In the distance I saw the hunkering form of the big Brumby King, fat and black as night. It was circling a Silver Peterbilt. The sound was like wildfire roaring, and a screech like no human throat has ever passed. Blast of air horn. I snuggled into Isa and she was there too. The Brumby King crashed up against the silver, which bucked, wheels spinning as it slid around. The Silver whined and fishtailed away. It didn't want it just yet and the Brumby King couldn't force it. They tracked around each other in a slow circling dance, the booming beats rising up from the Brumby King's sound system. Silver wasn't gunna let the King in so easy, but the King was used to this game it seemed. It closed fast and sudden, they were right beneath us and Silver didn't have nowhere to go. We saw everything as the Brumby King jammed itself against Silver, sparks flying from the panels. Silver was ready now, it scooted out from the side of the Brumby King, but then stood still. I could almost see the quivering and the shaking through the chassis. The King made a run up to a rocky ledge to get some air and mount up on Silver's back axle. Silver bucked and revved its donk but the King crashed home. The two trucks was locked together now and the fierce gunning of donks settled slower as they moved as one in the smokey desert air. Silver were ready to receive the King now and with a grunt of its donk it cummed out its load into the dust. Even far away I smelt it sharp and clean as the smell of solvents and diesel fuel on the breeze.

Something happened to Isa, she was softer then. She was turned on by the truckrutting. A skew of little droans scampered out to where the Brumby King pumped its seed to gather it up and take it inside. Of course the trucks couldn't mate like animals, so they'd got some helpers along to carry the parts. I put me arm around Isa and me face into her neck, smelling her earthy scent, it made me high. By this time Silver calmed down. It had come back in closer while the Brumby King took off now that it'd spent its load. The droans skittered around and with their feelers they gathered up the King's issue and carried it inside the Silver. They were making a babby truck, mechin together their separate parts into a newmint truckmind for a substrate that would find a truckbody one day. But I was lost in the moment, feeling Isa up close, reaching inside her trucksuit and me mouth searching for hers, pressing closer and she closed her eyes and yielded. I felt her small teats and reaching further down, pulled the suit down and ripped at me own zippers too and the roar of the brumbies fell into the background as I fell into Isa. I was hard as stone and she was sopping wet between her legs and I slid in all of a rush of blood going to me head, blood storming through me veins. Isa's voice caught in her throat as she took me and I bucked like that Brumby King till I cummed me load out inside her and the colours flared behind me eyes.

*

We laid together in the afterglow and this is the yarn Isa told: 'The folks what lived in the gigacity, they had everythin any one could want. They had all the knowin of machines and truckin lanes and their world was a massive system what ran almost by itself. It became almost its own livin thing until the real livin things started on dyin all around them. Somethin happened to the system and it stopped workin in some places and then more and more the machines was breakin down and leavin the slave grid to look after them selfs. And the ground poisoned the machines and they started doin their own thing with no thoughts of the system of the gigacities. And the gigacities was poisoned too and now there's no one that goes there. That's how the people came to live in the scattered camps in the backroads lookin to the Wotcher for answers and a way to get back to the past.'

I was just lying there looking into her eyes as she spoke. I didn't want it to end. Her voice was soft and flowing like the sounds of a creek. She went on.

'The Wotcher's got its place in two worlds. It's from the world of the past and the knowin system of seedin the gigacities but it speaks into the world of the backroads and the machines like flapples and robodogs. It's a bridge. That's why it's so important and I wunna crack the Wotcher's secret. Coz it's got the knowin in there somewhere of how to reseed the system of them buildins what talk to each other grow together and generate the power of the world. Underneath all the bullshit, there's the truth in the Wotcher of the past and if we can figure out the knowin we can find our way back to balance. Not like now where it's all down to muscle and how much weight you can pull. But Smoov ain't gunna give me the codes till he thinks I've earnt the right. Well I got a different idea coz there's new kinds of life comin up outta the ground, you seen it in the slinky snake what bit me. It's changed me, I can feel it. There's a cracklin in the air whenever Smoov hits the linkmaker. I can almost hear the Wotcher in me own head now. I'm seein things more clear. Once I get the last codes of the Wotcher and I can hook with the right roadin crowd, hybrid animal or machine and I know it's only a matter of time before I can lead the backroads folks to return to the gigacities. Smoov don't like them thoughts though. Plus he never trucked with no notions of the Wotcher as a saver, he never thought the Wotcher were anythin but a messenger sent to message us with ways to make our lives better. It's things everyone knowed all ready any way, he would just put them so as to be new and understandable.'

I was taken in by her voice and thoughts formed up in me mind.

I said, 'Why don't we go see the gigacities? We could find them and live a new life with them. Anyway we would have better chances by our selfs.'

'Gigacities is poisoned ground now. No one goes there. And I still gotta lot to learn from Smoov for showin.'

'He's gunna go too far one time and I'm gunna get too hurt to road. If I stay I'm gunna die.'

'I'm gunna be showman some day. I like you, Jon Ra, but if you're gunna leave, I won't stop you.'

I let her talk on a bit but inside I was dying. I knew then she was never gunna leave while Smoov was alive, no matter what she thought of a life with me. I dragged me feet in the sand behind as we trudged back to the camp for the show.

Chapter 7

When we got back, there was a bloke dressed in rags with a horse's mane sewed into his cowl. He was chanting to the crowds. They were listening to him, he was calling them. We stood and heard as he told a story about a man with a horse's head and black holes for eyes.

'The prophet come in to town walkin talkin wonderment and the folks that seen him ran in fright from his fearsome head and his strange talk. He was a prophet spreadin the word. He said, "There's gunna come a hand of fate to wash the sand from yer eyes and lift yer up outta the dust. You don't hafta wait for patterns to form or listen to the showmans no more." The horse's head said it came to tell of a saver from the Wotcher that will save the backroads folks out from the brumbies and the disorder.'

One fella piped up from the crowd, 'How come he got a horse's head?'

'He got the horse's head coz horses is strong and faifull, he were a strong and faifull bloke. He had a mate ship too and he sailed the desert backroads with his mates, they was lookin for the Wotcher's word from where it crackled. They heard the Wotcher was gunna come down to earth, it'd land like a flapple on a carcass and out would step a bloke who'd be a saver for us all from the brumby trucks.'

Smoov came on the scene then. He said, 'Wotcher's not somethin to be a saver. Wotcher's got messages in patterns and lessons for us all to make a better life, that's all. There's no saver. Theres no bloke with a horse's head, no mate ship in the desert, just a bloke tellin porky pies to serve himself.'

'You think you're a truth sayin servant of the Wotcher? Whaddaya know of it?' said the preacher.

The crowd grumbled and mumbled, faces showing dark at Smoov.

'I listen the Wotcher every night. I been puttin together the Wotcher's signs and meanins for twenty-six wet and twenty-six dry and mate I tell you, the Wotcher's no saver. It's a link to the past but it don't care what goes on. It's just spinnin high up above and sendin down messages to show a way of livin that's better than all this, that's all.'

The preacher shook his horsey mane and said, 'There's a mob of brumby trucks massin on the outside. They're gunna come in and ride over everythin inside. All they want is death and destruction. We don't need no truth nor lies nor messages. We need a saver from the brumbies.'

There were more murmurings from the camp folks. They were getting restless now. They'd been listening to Smoov a long time but their grumblings were for the idea of a saver. Smoov weren't having no part of it.

He turned and said, 'Wotcher's the one thing left from them as what come before, it's a key but we don't know the right door to open. If you listen the Wotcher, you can see there's something to take away, you can see the message. There's patterns that form in the trancemissions, and there's truth in them patterns.'

I looked at Isa.

'What you reckon?' I whispered.

'The preacher bloke's runnin his own program. He's tryin to get the folks to believe in a saver to lift himself in their eyes and become more powerful. There's many truths to the Wotcher and we've gotta make up our own minds about it. We gotta be our own savers, or maybe it's me what can be the saver if I can crack the Wotcher's code. I reckon the horse's head bloke is a sign the high breds are comin into the world.'

Right then there was some wrestling and wrangling going on. People were getting rowdy, they didn't like that Smoov were disrupting the show. They'd got a new showman in who was giving them something they wanted to hear. They were sick of Smoov and the other showmans who wouldn't ever give them nothing they could understand. Someone called: 'Git outta here, Smoov. Yer not welcome tonight.'

I thought Smoov was gunna chuck a wobbly, but he stood up straight and said, 'I been comin for years. Youse know my comin and goins, I always do a good show for yer needs, show for meat and smoke and cactusflower grog. I know the ways of the truck and the road and I've been givin youse suckle on the Wotcher's teat all this time.'

One of the camp blokes pushed forward. He was long scraggly hair and beard hanging down over hessian coat. 'Smoov, there's more to the Wotcher than what you can show. This bloke with the horse's head, what word come into the camps around two months ago, he's got a different story to tell. We wunna hear it. You can't stop it, even if you don't like it.'

'Be careful of this horse's head bloke, he's sick, he's crook with a evil virus. He's given you tell what you wanna heer, not the hard work of the roadin highways.'

Temper Storm the head man moved up then and said: 'Best off now, Smoov. Take yer kin and move it on.'

'It's gloomin darker, Temper, and we gotta show to do. We won't be roadin now.'

'Yes yer will, Smoov, yer gunna cause trouble if ya stay. I'm gunna give yer meat and smoke for the way, but yer on yer own now. Don't come back around next time.'

Smoov wrinkled his face up and went to move the show gear.

'Orright, Temper, I heer ya. I'm takin me childers and I'm headin off and I won't be back and now there's not gunna be no more shows for this camp.'

He sort of stopped a bit, waiting for someone to say he should stay. But there weren't no one said nothing.

'Suits us, Smoov,' said Temper. 'Road and be well.'

I thought Smoov was gunna do his block but he didn't. He just turned tail and walked. The crowd closed in around him and I caught a glance of the preacher's smug smiling face as the camp thronged around him to hear the messages of a saver.

There was an alarm right then, from the watch tower. The brumbies we saw that afternoon were massing for a raid and I thought on that Brumby King and what it wanted, and it's hard to know how to defend against something like that, almost like trying to work out what a thunderstorm might want or why. It just was. It swallowed up everything in its track and doused it with death and like a thundercloud, it didn't have no thoughts for what was left behind in the mud and the blood. So the camp folks were keeping their eyes out for that dust cloud, the sign of the Brumby King and its roading mob. They'd built fences and ditches and they'd hammered spikes into the road around, facing out. They'd laid grease traps and they'd buried bombs besides the road. But seeing that cloud on the skyline sent me cold. I don't wanna ever see it again. It was the brumby mob moving fast, off road.

They weren't coming in along the track where we saw them earlier. They were coming from the waste to lay waste. And then on the other side of the camp was another mob. In the brumbies were six rigs, led by the black beefy Brumby King itself and the new wrangled Silver Peterbilt next to it. Then there come the Left Tenant, white and blue and another blue on blue and the rest of the brumby mob followed by a crowd of droans buzzing about in their wake looking for whatever they could scab.

Looking closer at the other mob I could see it was just two indies roading. They weren't part of the brumby mob, but they were gunna get caught up in the storm of the Brumby King. One red and white and one with purple patterning, roading partners roaming free. Their path was getting crossed with the brumby mob right in front of the camp. I stood watching, I couldn't take me eyes off what was happening. The indies didn't realise the threat of the brumbies or they thought they could take them, because they didn't change course until it was too late and the brumbies were all around. The Brumby King took a fancy to the purple and so it crashed up against it while the Left Tenant and the other brumbies circled around and kept the red and white busy. The King wasn't mucking around trying to mount with its donk, it wanted to wrangle the purple into its mob. Even though the red and white done its best to drive off the King, it was overwhelmed and outnumbered. It drove off by itself, to the westing while the King and its mob pressed on.

Watching from the fence, the greasy camp boys went pale.

There wasn't nothin no one could do, it was just a matter of time before they'd be on us.

'Carn,' I said to Isa, 'we gotta move.'

'Wheres Smoov?'

'He's gone to sling his tote from the showgear. There's no time, we gotta go.'

'I'm not leavin till he's given me the codes so as I can show in me own right. Anyways we would be killed out in the open.'

Maybe she was right but I didn't wanna stick around, I felt the pull in me guts. We would die if we stayed. We had to go, but we'd already done too much talking, the heat was coming down. The first shots of rocks were falling down, launched like missles from the brumby trucks, they were raining pain and stone and shards of bone.

A crash right next to us and a brumby busted through the fence, wheels jarring through the shocks, engine screaming, dust flying, rocks falling and folks were running to get away. The panic hit me. I grabbed Isa's arm but she still wouldn't come. She pulled away and I just had to run to save myself. The air throbbed with the beating of battling trucksound, steady bass rumbling and horns tweeting and dripping with jammy delay.

The Left Tenant came on hard, howling and screaming diff and high pitched turbine whine cutting through the deep rocking grumble sound of the donk. And then it blasted a tune, a cranking dub that whipped the following brumby mob into a frenzy of high revving engines and the blat blat blat of exhaust brakes. Up come the Left Tennat's own second, light blue frag patterns on dark blue, its vents wide open under blank view screen sensors as it sucked up all the air around to cool its searing manifold. Once they'd busted through the fence, they went all different ways through the camp looking for damage and destruction. The noise was terrible, dust and smoke in me throat and every breath was hard won from the thickening air. Camp folks screaming in panic and fetching up their gear, whatever could be carried. A dog ran past snarling and snapping, fear inside its eyes but angry outside.

Through the dust and smoke and bodies rushing here and there, all of a sudden I came face to face with Smoov, his eyes wild. He made to grab me arm and pull me back with him and I didn't say nothing. It all happened so fast I just wanted to be done with it. All them pent up feelings came rushing out, Brumby King or not, I wasn't gunna go with Smoov no more. I stepped sideways as he over reached and he fell into the space where I used to be and then fell down onto his knees. Between Smoov and the blur of moving bodies behind, I saw Crow. He wore a coat made from trucktyre and he had silver hair but you could see as how it had been black as night and his brown face was lined and white eyes that he looked in me eyes with a glare and I knew we were tied together on the roading. Fear hit me like cold water gulped too fast and settled in me guts, wanting to loosen me stools. The face of Crow twisted sharp, it was cold and hard like broken brick.

'Do it,' Crow said.

Smoov was down on his knees in front of me, he looked sidewise up and the sweat beaded on his face and runned down his neck. He didn't say nothing, like he knew what was inside me, what he'd given me the power over him to do. Crow said: 'Carn, you barstid. Otherwise you got buckleys of havin it off with the girl.'

He spat the end of his durry into the red dirt. In the chaos a moment of still. The jenny's throb and the clear blue sky and high white cloud. Wind blowed from the east, sun overhead and way, way up a flapple rode updrafted. Folks moaned and dogs barked and the brumby mob ran them down and crying mouths were crushed under wheels till they didn't cry no more. There was no home, no quiet place to shelter the storm. It was just whatever wits you had and I wished it was different but it weren't. I slit Smoov's throat with the shiv and seen the white line of fat under the skin before the red blood bubbled out and Smoov looked up into me face and gurgled but no sound came. Blood ran over his hands where he tried to hold it in over his new grin. He fell over onto his front and lay still while the red dust turned black.

Then I was looking around, Crow was nowhere. I scanned for a way out and I locked eyes with Isa.

She'd seen what I done.

I reached out to her but she turned and ran and I ran after her. She went straight into the path of the Brumby King humming

ANDREW MACRAE

up on the camp and in a second she was gone and the Brumby
King was gone in the dust and smoke and I was left in the wreck
of the camp with just the show gear, me typewriter and all the
notes and Smoov's linkmaker that I rummaged from his rags.
I shot through and cast in my lot as a rider.

Chapter 8

I crawled out of the camp on me belly through the scrub, cutting myself up on the sharp rocks and stones. Search lights swept around above, the trucks rolled in the distance and the air was full of howling sound. I breathed in dust and sweated fearstink thumping heart. Sucked into this pathway like dust in the slipstream and swirling eddies in the air and rumblings in the ground. You can't say where that dust is going but it's pulled along even though one minute ago it was just sitting by the side of the road.

Isa lost, almost like she was sucked up by the air around the Brumby King. Nothing but the smell of smoke and the ash of me thoughts that I sifted through to find the things that'd gone wrong in me life. Core of an apple with a maggot. Isa wet where I touched her. It was all gone, the brumbies came and smashed up everything and I was roading lonely now. The dreams of a life with Isa on the show circuit were smashed up like Smoov's showgear. Broken like the bone broken faces in the camp during the raid. And the only thing I could think was how I had to find Isa. It was the only way I could make things right again. She was missing, lonely too, probably injured and hurting and Wotcher only knows what that Brumby King wanted with her.

I came to a ditch and I crawled along it till it turned into a roadside drain. There was a bloke in there wrapped in a blanket, white eyes open and flashing the dark. We whispered at each other as the rumbling rigs passed by all around.

'I don't want no trouble,' he said.

'Me neither, can I share yer hideyhole?' I said.

'You can share but I got nothin for you to use.'

'I'm the same.'

Thumping pounding of brumby wheels rocked the ground. A flash of light lit the hole and his eyes were open wide. He saw me tote and the typewriter case and I said,

'It's just a old machine for wordin.'

He shook with fear and I was shook too. Taste of dust and tyre smoke from the burning camp thick in me throat.

'I don't want nuthin to do with this. I'm just passen through, ay,' he said.

'Mate I know it I lost me sis–'

A brumby skitter flickered past the opening and we shut up in the darkness. The grambling and hummering of the trucks rumbled outside. They shone their lights flickering around the drain close by. Time stetched out before us. The sounds slackened off after a while and he whispered, 'They's gunna be roadin like this all night?'

'I dunno. Reckon they'll probly head off once they've got done with their raidin and the skitters and droans has looted everything what can be taken.'

'They took yer sis?'

'I think she's been took by the Brumby King.'

He went quiet for a bit then he said: 'You sure she's not dead?'

When he said that, I were chilled. I said: 'Na, no way. That'd never happen to Isa, she's tough and trucksmart. I saw pretty clearly she was gone into the smoke left behind by the Brumby King.'

He gave me a look like I were a sad sap and we curled up against the cold night while those trucks tore up the road above and the cloying piss stink closeness kept us safe.

Dawn came up, he were gone with his dirty blankets and the trucks had moved on. There were birds calling, daylight bleeding into the sky against a smudge of black smoke from the camp.

That morning I rememberd the time I lost me Mum and Smoov come along and picked me up from me misery into more misery. His face scritchy and his stinking breath and Isa was there too. The memory of her eyes locked on to mine. Thinking of that memory of Isa's eyes set me blubbering, like maybe I'd never see her again. I let go of everything I'd been holding onto so tight in the night as I ran from the brumbies. Let go of what I'd done to Smoov, the flash of his fear right before I killed him, and the way he tried to talk though his throat was slit. It's a bad feeling, knowing you've done something like that, but I didn't have no choice if I wanted to be with Isa.

And anyway there wasn't nothing for it but to get back out to the road so that's what I done. I crawled out through the spinifex and put the red dust green grey mountains in the back of me and the easter sun in me face, same way the tracks of the brumby mob headed. And if I could track down that Brumby King I could find Isa and we could live a life together on the show circuit.

I could feel a following behind, I saw its cloud of dust and I knew in me heart it was the same thing that followed us in to Hind Pass and it'd been following me since we fled from the brumbies in the gorge. Maybe longer. Maybe it wasn't after Smoov at all. Anyway, nothing I can do about the past so I roaded without looking behind. Felt the glare of those following eyes on the back of me trucksuit. In the wasted land I sopped up water from stinking sinkholes, moving from one to the next along the lay lines that had been in use for longer than humans walked on two legs. No food for days but that was all right, I could live off me own body a while so long as I had water. Looking for a mount, looking for anything that could speed my passage through that blasted flatscape of dry cunt creekbed and thorny prick termite nest stickin up from the ground on the trail of the brumbies that fled to the east. You can't live long out there if you don't got some knowing of the desert and Smoov taught us how to read the signs and rig a snare for rabbits. So come dusk and the red sun sinking I found a warren and snared up a mangy old doe. Skinned and dressed and chewed raw, sweet blood and strips of red flesh. I didn't wanna risk a fire and I were that hungry it didn't bother me none. Laid down underneath a truckdream of stars in the void, lonely as a flea on a salt pan. Tried to hide myself as best I could.

I woke dead of night, no more moon, stars shifted around all wrong and there it was, the follower, right in front of me eyes. Its face was bleached white bone, its eyes were white, it had a crooked beak and a black hoodie over its head. In the black dot in the centre of the eye I saw me own face reflected back at me. It wore a trucktyre coat and when it opened its mouth it let out a croak. In its hand it had a cloth bag and it held the bag out for me. I felt me own hand reaching out and going into the bag though it was the last place I could think of where I'd wanna put me hand. Inside was little rattling things, dry like wood. I pulled one out and looked at it and the creature clacked and croaked some more and I saw that dried up bone in me hand, a backbone of some creature, smaller than a man but bigger than a dog. There was a mark carved in black on that bone and I saw it was an /I/.

Next thing I knew it was dawn and I was soaked in sweat, a fever in me head and no idea of whether it was a dream or otherwise. I'd not seen them bones before, nor the sign and I puzzled on it as I moved me aching body onwards under the cover of low clouds sweeping across from the north. It was an /I/ like that /I/ that stared out from my /eye/ but wasn't /eye/ nor /I/. It was an /I/ reflected in an /eye/, the dead bone eye of the creature, the follower. The Crow. It was also the /I/ for /Isa/ and that's the sign I took it for as the day moved and I moved through it knowing which direction to go but not where my fate lay. I came to a road and I figured that would be as good a place as any to sit for a time and recover myself. No sign of the follower. It'd taken what it wanted for now, moved me own hand somehow just by freezing me there in the moment.

Clouds burnt off and it got hot but I stayed at the roadside puzzling on me dream or whatever it was. There was a rumbling from the distince and a bright spark of sunflash on metal. Me heart thumped in me ribs, it was an indie for sure, heading east like I was. I pulled Smoov's linkmaker from the tote where I'd stowed it with the typewriter. I waved a link through the air like I seen Smoov do, me head rushing with the thought this could be me first truckride solo.

The truck must have seen me wave and it ground down the gears as it slowed. It stopped long enough for me to climb up, but it wasn't an indie at all. It was a dumb slavegrid hauler left from the oldtimes heading on the tracks between the camps and it wouldn't let me into the cab. It was just gunna keep on going when it saw I didn't have nothing ready to trade but I swung up on the back anyway. Me first truckride spent in an open air trailer. There wasn't nothing wild about it, nothing like what I'd expected it would be when I was young and listening to the riders tell their stories round the campfires. Outside the night air rushed past in a cold clear blast and underneath the road clattered by. The slavegrid truck wasn't on the link freek no more but it let me stay because I was there then and the darkness came down on me though there weren't no truckdreams just blackness and emptiness of the end. When I woke there was another rider in there with me and I moved back away, wanting no company. A match flare lit the creases in his face and I saw it was Crow, same one as what talked to me that night in the camp, same one what waved to me when it was Smoov's turn. Same coat, but different from the creature in me dream. He took a toke off of his pipe and offered me some. I shook me head.

'Fancy seein you here,' he said.

'Yeah, fancy. You followin me now?'

'Sure you don't wanna toke? It'll ease yer pain,' he said.

'I'm not in any pain, mate.'

'Oh don't play the hard man with me, cobber. I know your type. Always in some kinda pain. Always got someone else to blame for what was done with yer own fists. Always lookin for some relief from the knowin of the blood on yer wrists.'

'You got me all wrong. I done nothin. I don't feel nothin,' I said.

'Ha ha, well be like that if you wanna, but this spike will

cure yer ails. One taste and she'll be apples.'

'I don't got no ails, I already told you. I don't want yer apples.'

'Try some of this. It's the juice from a stoned up indie true bred. They've always made the best gear, to tempt the riders who'll give em the best patches.'

He moved closer, I pushed him away but he grinned and pulled his spike.

'Carn, it's good shit.'

And in the darkness I just wanted to lose myself from all that'd happened, so I took the spike. The truckdream held onto me through the cold night and the thoughts I had of Isa kept me going. I knew through it all I was getting closer to her on the easting road and with the haze humming in me veins, I felt I was getting closer to putting the pieces of bone together into a whole. I thought of the first time I saw inside of something, I felt the pull of it on me eyes, downwards. I couldn't look away. It was a roadkilled dog. Freshly dead and glistening it was, flies shiny and black on the bright red. A spray of blood from its mouth where it coughed up its last. Blue and yeller guts spilled out for all to see, the inner secrets of life all spread out in the dust and gravel. Dead eyes empty and wide and white in fear, and I knew: all creatures know death that comes in the dark and takes the light from a life. Everyone's scared when it's their turn. Some run towards it and if you don't know how to live, maybe it's a way out. Little beating heart pumped all its life out onto the ground.

Chapter 9

Next day and I was grimy from the truckride, blood behind me eyes. Blood in me dreams, creatures in me dreams, skeletons and bleached bones of animals that have never been nor never could be, animals made up in someone else's mind, a slaved truck with a load of scared riders pushing through the night, riders on the way to slaughtering in the maw of the road. And there was nothing at all to it, just the smooth flow of the surface with nothing beneath it neither. It was all just words wrote out of order on this typewriter I found.

I came out of me dream lying roadside where the truck stopped for watering, wasted and bruised from that spike and laid out underneath the water tower in the morning sun. All I had was me tote and typewriter with all of Smoov's notes in the lid, his linkmaker and a cell of jenny juice saved up to slot the substrate when it fades. Me mouth full of broken and rotted teeth. I knew I had to find a tasty rig to roll with if I stood any chance of catching up with the brumby mob. Their trail was going cold now, and I had to find Isa, it was pulling me along like a thread from the future. So I staggered to me feet. Sun to me face so I knew I must of been on the right road. Clouds from the past at my hind. Me tears didn't come, me eyes was dry as lies. The old life was dead and gone but sometimes there's some killing you have to do before you can become something new.

The road a straightedge rule bordered with bodies of cars and bodies of burnt out trucks and bodies of roos. Those roads were tough on vehicles as well as roadkill. Every little bit used up, bones picked clean. Same as with the machines come to scavenge too, looking for parts or even a whole new body to mech with a new truckmind. I saw one in there, an old Kenworth foraging sad in the wreckage almost out of juice. Old trucks turning back to dust, it's the cycle, isn't it? But there's ways to find bits of yourself in new bodies. We are all made from the same stuff, it's come from the stars in the night sky and that's where it's all gunna go in the end and meantimes it's sure to come back around. Your body knows all this, even if your head don't, like those feelings you've seen something before but you know you ain't never, or when you meet someone and it's like you've known them your whole life and you just slot right in. Or how some folks can try their hands at something and they pick it up real quick, like how Isa just took to the show and tell, she had done it before she were Isa, I knew it. There's another world trying to break through into this busted one. If only it could, that would be something to see. Maybe things would be better than they is now. Maybe that's what Isa was on about, trying to find the bridge between the two worlds.

I walked the lonesome road, waiting for the right ride. That first truckride trailer was a balls up, and I was still sickened from the spike of hazy truckdream, but it was a seed planted. Somewhere on some level I knew I wanted more. Feeling sick and feeling like Isa's disappearing further and further away with each wasted hour. Pretty soon there was a rumbling and a grumbling and a dust cloud blowed up in the west. I flipped the freeks and found the source, it was an indie for sure and this time I was ready with a patch file from Smoov's list. The truck tasted the patch I blinked over to it, something that would buzz its truckmind the way the haze buzzed mine. It was coming slower and slower until I saw it, a red and white rig. It grew in me eyes, something to behold, its rocking power and the size of it. Then I felt its heat as it came in for a stop and idled right beside me. It was tricked with patchwork glyphs and sygils patterning messages from mysterious places and I saw a name written in curly writing: /Sinnerman/. I realised then it was the same rig that lost its mate to the Brumby King in the raid that also took Isa. The King had driven off with that other one glyphed Storm and something in me said Sinnerman was on this same road as me for a reason. Something in me made me want to touch it, so I got up close as it hummered there. I smelled the air around, alive with newmint particules and longchain polymers, breathed it all in in a big giddy swallow.

Me hand reached out without me doing anything to move it and I watched as I touched smooth metal skin, felt the cool surface and it seemed to move under me touch from the vibrations of the donk. I sighed, and then Sinnerman gunned it, grumbling thunder from deep inside and it moved away, circled around and came back, blowing black smokestack exhaust. A beat started up and the wave rocked with its sounds. I calmed me breathing and reached out with me mind through the link, touching something in the freek, feeling in me head the shape of that light, those sounds.

Perfect timing, perfect play of the link, you have to get it just right as the indie is coming up the road. Too soon and they'll bolt, too long and, well, it's a matter sometimes also of just letting them get used to you. Use to yeour sweatstink, your human ways. I talked in a soft whisper, low in me throat, soothing. It just came natural. Dunno how you're meant to soothe a machine, they've got programs of their own, but if they can see your no threat at least you can get started. That's how it was with Sinnerman. I just put me bag down and sat in the dust and shuffled patches through the link, shifting through different cycles. Though it was flighty and wanted to be roading after its mate, it was also curious to see what I was up to, see what patches I'd come up with. It wanted a rider for this road and maybe it sensed I was roading after the Brumby King for the same griefstruck reasons. I found a nice combo between two different patch sets, tweaking its inner runnings the way haze or cactusflower grog tweaks a human brain, and soon it settled down. I blinked a new patch and tried to tempt it, but it thrummed away again, spewing smoke from the stack. I calmed myself and thought of how Smoov would of done it in his chats with indie trucks, but thoughts of Smoov didn't really help with calm. Just a wave of fear and guilt but I put it to one side and tried again.

Another patch, called Skull Deth. It seemed to speak from the list, something about it, so I tried that one on and the indie pricked up its whole body and started to shake and shimmer. I stood there as that massive machine came right up to me, growling engine vibrating into the ground and through me body. It glowed with power. I put out me hand to touch its cold steel flank again and it moved even closer to get more of a whiff of that Skull Deth in its link. Smell of nothing, scent of always moving freeways and blue sky dreams. Shifting in those sands. Me heart fast and loud in me ears to be so close to my first true indie truckride, and it was a fucken bewdy, too. Red and white steel glimmering in the daylight. No load nor trailer, wild and free. Like I wished I could be. Well I blinked the Skull Deth through the link and Sinnerman settled right down. It opened up the hatch for me to climb in. I put me foot on the first chrome rung and climbed up to the rider's cab.

Inside was a little womb. Warm and cozy, with a stink of mixed human and machine. Padded couch made for one or maybe two riders. Viewscreen that showed you the world all around, plus whatever the truck wanted to show you. And then near the left hand side, down low, there's the IV rig where you can slot your spike, you can jack right in and feel the flow of the haze as the truck cranks the feedline from its alkaloid synthfac and you're one with the machine as it's gaining speed. I patted the dash and said: 'Me and you, we're on the same road now, we got the same program. We're gunna chase down the Brumby King and I'll help you get back your mate and we can find Isa together as well and then it'll all be sweet.'

Sinnerman gunned its engine and we started rolling, and Sinner seemed like it was happy to have a rider. Maybe it seen Isa be taken, like I'd seen Sinner's mate Storm herded off, and we were on the same wavelength to chase down the brumby mob. While maybe I needed a ride more than Sinnerman needed a rider, there were times a handy dose over the link from a rider could help a truck along on its mission. I slotted the spike.

It came on dirty at first, nothing so clean, but soon I was grinning and smiling, me jaw tight and clenched though I was loose. I shook another dose of Skull Deth from the link, and Sinnerman floored it, I felt the feedback through the line, a different note in my own high as the tyres bit down on black road. I could feel the vibes in me whole body, up through me arse and into me chest, me mind was raging with the high of wrangling a wild indie and the high of jacking some haze straight from the source. It was me and the road and Sinnerman, I was trying to get used to how the link worked, trying to bend me will to the truck's innerface but not having much luck. We were rolling and I wasn't scared of no follower, I just wanted some clear air behind and maybe some mountains out of the desert in front, and on the road to where I could find Isa.

Through the little hatch into the rider's cab, it was a warm dark place and soft with light coming from a strip at the front. It was safe and it smelled close with body heat of riders past and roadsmell, solvents and oil and exhaust and woodsmoke and something else, something what come off the glimmering tech those trucks made themselves, polymers and particules and the smell of raw haze. High tech and still fallen, remains of a system that didn't work the way it should any more, so it'd taken off on its own pathway. I roaded with Sinnerman, out to the end of the line. The highway unwound ahead, white line a call sign dragging me along through the swirling dust and the surly memories. Up high in the rider's cab, high as a flapple's eye in Sinnerman's insides. I cranked haze and slotted home the rusty IV jagged like a nail, dead like lead but alive with signs and meanings and the wind was singing outside. It was all black in the dark of night but in the cab I was at peace not pieces. I was at one with the road being eaten up underneath the wheels.

We roaded eastly coastwise towards a burnt out desert truckstop and I tried to get Sinnerman to slow so we could check for signs of brumby passing, but I realised with a shock I'd got no hold over the indie truck. It was feisty and it just wanted to keep going on. It didn't even hardly feel the feeble tug I could manage on the linkmade patches. I shuffled files to see what I could get it to do. No dice, nothing. I felt a rise of panic, I didn't realise it were gunna be like this to road with an indie. Getting to the truckstop suddenly seemed vital, if I was gunna prove my will over Sinnerman. I popped the hatch and made to jump. It was all I could do to show Sinnerman that I was serious, but it did at least start to slow as we come up to the truckstop. Though it wanted only one thing, to go after Storm. I didn't know how to tell it that we'd need to collect signs to the roading along the way, that we'd have to stop from time to time to check the trail. I slotted another patch designed to cool it down and it snorted and blared its exhaust brakes to a stop just past the truckstop. Picking through the ruins, there were nothing much more than a burnt out shell, black pools of plastic melted hard into liquid shapes. Cables and cords hung down from the stripped out ceiling. In one corner all the furniture was piled and in the shadows of the shell it looked like some kind of sickened robo. Crunching on broken glass under me feet and through the wrecked kitchen to the workshop at back. There wasn't nothing there neither, but in the mess left on the work bench was a geo grid patchfile and when I blinked it through the linkmaker I saw we were close to Midden Dump. That rung true, the Midden Dump had all the right tags and if my instincts were right, it would be a magnet for brumbies and other indie trucks.

Back in the cab, I felt the fear of what was left behind and the longing for Isa that laid ahead. Sinnerman was in the zone too, I cranked a new patch, something that I'd seen Smoov messing with and I felt a fluttering feeling in me guts and the truck moved underneath a shift and a squirt as it rolled along, travelling faster and faster. Opened the throat of the throttle, road hiss sucking sound from the air and the patch in the flow of haze from the IV. A shift in the note of the throbbing rush that beat through the link and inside the cab was its own little world, roading after Isa. I slumped into myself and the stars washed out and it all turned black and I slept safe like a babby in its Mum's arm.

Chapter 10

The highway to the Midden Dump was all choked with traffic. Trucks and mangled vans and clattering wrecks of barely moving vehicles and camels and horses and mules pulling carts made out of the rearends of cars. Skitters skated around and fed off a dead truckbody while a two leg droan stumped past on the track and flapples flew in the sky. Further on and two bigdog robos ate at a roadkilled roo. Blokes on horseback and blokes with guns and blokes with grinning faces in dresses and hats, and women with babbies and women with knifes in their teeth and women fire twirling, all heading to the place where all creatures went to gorge off the rotted carcass of the whole world. And somewhere in there in all that mess I was sure I'd find someone who could tell me where the Brumby King was at. Brumbies would be drawn to that place like moths into the show light. And maybe there we would find the road to Isa. Isa, like ice. Still, like a frozen river in the mountains when winter came. I saw it in a dream in Sinnerman's truckcab, coming out of the darkness in the headlights. She was there or somewhere close, I knew it and I felt it in me bones.

It was a grey dawn and smoke blew in the wind. Traffic was thicker the closer we got. The heat cranked up, buzz of biz, only one road in and one road out. Trucks carted loads in and trucks carted loads out. There were trucks piled high with all the garbage brought from the bottom of the ruined camps and the corners of the gigacities and the data mines. It was all the stuff of the old times being rebirthed up into the new world through the movements of the trucking lanes and the arsehole of the earth. All the world's garbage was drawn there by magical forces, and I wondered what the folks expected to do with that trash but even at the end of the world there was a market for everything. There were folks who made their whole lives out of garbage. Roadside thickened up with more and more shacks and hovels and then we rounded a turn and I saw in the distance the mountain that was Midden Dump. It were futher east than I'd ever been, though I'd heard many stories about it. Smoov's show circuit never wound that far.

The traffic heavy, but it moved along and soon the mountain was all I could see of earth and sky, blocking out the morning sun. We were well and truly coming up on the centre of things, the shacks were more solid, there wasn't no structures, no order nor nothing but still it was a city built of plastic and canvas and peopled with scavengers. The trucks dropped off their loads and turned around as people and machines crawled over each other to be the first at it. And it was being picked over by the crows and the packs of dogs and robos scrounging parts, trying their best to get by. And there were all kinds of people there too, showmans picking through all the bits, mining for data, and truck mechs lookin for secrets of the patch and there were just plain hungry folks searching for whatever they could find to eat. Eating off each other, eating off roadside weeds and cactusflower, eating off corpses, eating off dirt. Goanna cult on show, perengi march crossing the road, traffic frozen on all sides for the beast that was seven hands tall at the shoulder. It was painted with signs and sigils like a truck would be. It wasn't shackled but jewelry hung around its neck on chains. Goannaman out front and white clad followers shuffling behind. The lizard rolled slow and easy not a quick skitter like out in the desert. That thing was a King and it knew it, too. The traffic still blocked, stopped dead. Sinnerman was antsy to be roading after its lost partner and the Brumby King but there was nothing it could do. There was no way through so I said, 'I'm gunna go in on foot, see if there's any word of those brumbies.' Even though Sinnerman couldn't understand a word.

I hitched Sinnerman through the link and it parked, chewing on a heavy narco patch I'd found, and I reckoned that would keep it quiet while I was out and about. I had a quick rush of feeling, hoping Sinner wasn't gunna run before I got back because if the patch wore off too quick I had a feeling it would get on the way without me. But I swung on down anyway, into the crush and the swell of all those bodies. The smell hit, raw sweet, sour, the smell of death. The smell of bushsmoke and exhaust and fumes, smell of rotted flesh and spent fuel cells and bodies and cooking oil. Tang of piss and cloy of shit. It were all around. There was no easy way through so I clamped on me dustmask and I put myself right into it.

Right away I seen a bigdog robo feeding off a lizard carcass and folks walking like it was nothing new or wrong with a robo eating meat. Funeral smoke in the air, blokes carried bodies on their shoulders to the burning ground. Movement and sound, ashes flowed in the air like pieces of the sun's burnt husk falling to earth in front of me eyes. Grinning head of a stoned showman pushing his cart through the muck. His eyes were gone far away and his hair a mass of dreads. Rusted steel machines on four legs, six legs, on tracks, on wing. Dirty and broken robos and black crows flapped nearby. Past a white shed, there were signs of an indie mob there, for sure. I could feel them in me bones. I could see it in the flash of light on steel body panel and through the space between piles of rubbish. Indie trucks, if not brumbies, and where there were indies there were sure to be brumbies not far off, because in the end they all needed the same things, patches and parts and panel work and coming together for a truck jam.

Before I came to the white shed though, I saw a bunch of grey faced folks sitting on their haunches picking dirt from besides a trash heap mound and rolling clumps of white clay into balls that they kept in woven plastic string bags. The dirt eaters' lazy and hollow eyes followed me with no sight to be seen. One bloke was lying on the ground and next to him his missus dug up the clay from the earth. Dug up scoops of it and put them in his mouth. She moved his jaws up and down but he couldn't swallow. They were men and women both, and now and then they put some clay into their mouth or the mouth of one of their kids while mangy dogs and busted robos hustled close to see, but those grey ghosts were the only ones who wanted the dirt. Even the animals were smart enough to know there was only suffering on that mound of clay. There was still some things that set humans apart from animals and machines and there was a cloud over those folks sleeping under blue tarps in the daylight and eating dirt that was just gunna kill them in the end. They were in some strange place in between, not living but not dead yet neither.

I was freaked out by the dirt eaters, they threw me off me game so I turned a little bit and took another pathway through the piles of rubbish where folks carted out loads and loads of copper wires from coils tore from the guts of machines and there was machines flappling around trying to get at the wires.

I said to one bloke, 'Anywhere round here I could score some haze?'

I knew that if there was haze, there'd be indies and maybe even brumbies.

He looked at me and larfed, 'Can't you see? It's all around. There's no shortage of it here.'

That was all he would say but I caught the flash of his eyes towards the white shed I'd seen before. I made back for the shed even though I'd just turned around. It stood out like dog's balls. It was now or never and as I came up to the inside of it, I saw a woman sitting down tending to the sick and wounded.

She was middle aged, and she had a sawed off shotgun on her knee but she was a healer I thought. No one would trouble her there, as long as she could do something for their needs. Which maybe she often couldn't, hence the gun. She wore clothes that actually fit, khaki pants and a shirt with shoulder tabs, and she had on glasses and her gray hair cut short to the scalp. She sat at a table making notes on a piece of paper, it were uncommon to see someone writing. There weren't many except for showmans who knew the ways of letters and signs. I was suddenly very curious about this woman.

Shuffling past the canvas door flap like I was a dump dweller, I found myself a spot where I could look and see but not be seen. There were bodies of dirt eaters on a slab inside the shed, their skin stretched over bone. I could hear her talking on the link in snatches: '…rotted faster than before,' and then, 'dead flesh is what the dump grows. There'll be no shortage come harvest.'

From the inside, I could see there were med supplies everywhere. That woman was a camp doctor for sure, and not like the medicine folk that healed Isa's snakebite. She knowed something of the old times healing powers. I found me balls and walked right through the door and up to her table.

'You've got writin tools?' I asked.

She looked at me through her specs, real quiet and long. Like she saw me for what I was and it weren't a nice feeling.

'What of it?'

'Well I'm real interested in writing. I been shown the basics of sounding words and letterin sentences. I'm writin down me own trancescrypts with this typewriter.'

I put up the HERMES up on the bench and she took a good look at it. Her whole face softened as she touched it, she suddenly opened up to talking to me.

'I've not seen one of these for a long time.'

'I use it to do me writin.'

The doctor looked closer at the pages snapped into the top of the case. She said, 'Maybe we're talkin about different kinds of writin.'

'What kinds is there?'

'There's the kind that tracks the comin and goin of stocks. That's what I do.'

'Well that's not so different really. I track me memories. Words once written down can't be changed like a memory will change.'

'True enough.' She picked at one of the keys and cranked a new line with the handle.

Another thought come to me and I said, 'Them words is tricky, but. They don't always act like I want em to and sometimes I reckon they hide the truth harder than if I'd not wrote em.'

'Written words're stuck in time and if you don't know the questions to ask em, all you'll hear back is your own thoughts,' she said.

I leaned over to look at the writing she was doing in her ledger what were bound in leather with ragged edges and the paper was smooth and creamy. She closed it so I couldn't see what was worded there.

'Keepin all the columns straight means I can tell where I'm with my biz.' Her eyes sharpened then. 'I bet that typewriter is good for keeping figgers in columns.'

I put the case back over the top of the HERMES. 'I dunno.'

'What do you want for it?'

I saw a opening then to find out more about brumby trucks.

I said, 'It don't seem right, this business of yours what you're trackin with columns and figgers.'

Her face darkened and I knew I hit a spot.

'Waddya know of my business? You're just a rider from the backroads.'

'Them dirteaters is the poorest of the poor and you're sellin their bodies to brumby trucks. They got nothin, they're eatin dirt.'

'Give me the typewriter and I'll tell you.'

'Tell me something I can use.'

'The white clay the dirteaters chew gives em some benefits but they die if they don't eat proper food. Their bodies don't rot because the clay has minerals that keep em from decomposing for a time. The brumbies take them and give me custom meds they can make in their synthfacs. I use them to treat the sick.'

'The dirt eaters are sick. Shouldn't you be healin em before they die?'

'There's nothin I can do for someone who won't help emself.'

'But you're helpin brumby trucks that don't care what they kill or steal to get what they want.'

She scoffed then. 'You're no better than they are in this world, rider, preyin on anyone weaker than yourself. Even with your typewriter and all your pretty lettered words, you're still just scavengin a life out of the road.'

That gave me a little pause. I said, 'Orright, you've told me a story. I'll give you this typewriter, but I need one more thing. I'm trackin down brumby trucks to find me sister, Isa. I gotta find her if I'm gonna find any peace in this life.'

This time the look she gave came over the tops of the glasses and she said, 'I think it's unlikely you'll ever find peace.'

I left that silence hanging there and she kept looking, looking through me like she knew me secret, seen me thoughts for Isa and the blood behind me eyes with Crow moving me hand against Smoov. Me face flushed up, I couldn't help it.

Then I said, 'At least gimme some idea as to where the brumby mob is hidin out.'

'Keep east, rider. And keep your eyes out to learn out more about what's goin on in the world before passin your judgements on others.'

She reached over to take the typewriter and I was gunna open me mouth to say fair enough, but then I saw a crow out of the corner of me eye. He hopped up on the shoulder of one of the dirteaters, and I took the typewriter and scampered. Her shotgun spat fire and smoke. Sting of rock salt bruised me arse and zipped past me ears and I ran from that white shed that was full of death, not healing.

Chapter 11

By the time I got back to Sinnerman it was dark and we roaded out of the dump and on through the night, shapes shifting white fog under the bright lights of the pumping rig, sticking to the east road still, towards where I thought the brumby mob would be travelling. That doctor knew something and the stink of brumbies was all around the Midden Dump but the trail dried up there. There were branching pathways and I had to take me best bet with the mountains up ahead and the easterling road towards the coast of the dead seas.

Grinding up a mountain range the next day. So many back tracks and dead ends, beating ahead to find a downed tree over the road and Sinnerman trying to push logs off the path. One thing about going that way, I could see there had not been no one through for a long time. I dunno what that meant exactly, whether it was good or bad. Good that we were not on any well travelled road, bad that we had no one to follow, just had to work it out from whatever fragments of maps I could piece together from the geogrid patchfiles I'd found in the desert truckstop. Make sure to keep the morning sun up in me face, even though the sun skirted a low track in the sky this time of year.

We kept on towards the coast, burning to get to the end. We had to find more trails of the Brumby King and I thought of Isa who was keeping me moving through that treacherous land of mist and tangled green trees growing all over everything. Last stretch over the top of the mountain, one more hump to go and the weather closed in, the wind blowed so cold and so fast off the cliffs. Sinnerman growled and yammered for a clear stretch of road but it was closed in on all sides and thundering coming from on high and lightening flashing. Another truck came barrelling round the bend towards us and we swerved over the road trying to find some grip but there was none, just mud. That truck was a half track, diesel, not even sentient, droved by a bloke with a baldy head and a red beard. I looked right into his eyes as he passed and seen through to the other side of him as if there wasn't nothing there against that black backdrop and the cold mountain air running in through the vents on me face. And then he was gone, but that vehicle had cut a track for us, so we followed it even though we didn't know where it was going. Comparing it with the geotags, there were sure signs it would take us to the other side of the mountain at least and soon enough we came across a track and then another and we followed it down to the wood cutters camp on the side of the mountain where maybe we could get something to eat and maybe some fuel juice for Sinnerman to top up its cells and swap some true lies road stories for word of the Brumby King.

We pulled in to a safe spot to stop and there was blokes all around, wherever I looked you seen them. They came out from the camp and crowded around Sinnerman. I didn't wanna let the fear stop me so I unjacked and climbed down. Maybe they'd have word of brumbies because far as I could know the trail had gone cold.

They were dressed in animal skins, no tech among them from their looks and they were looking at the truck in wonderment. Well it was no surprise, it was a wonderful thing to behold. One old bloke reached out to touch it.

'Bonza truck you got there, mate,' he said.

'Hands off,' I said.

He looked down on the ground. A young bloke came up, eyes full of stars.

'What kind of truck is it? Got any haze on yer?'

Ah so that was what was gunna get me in with them.

'I doubt youse would of ever seen a fine indie truck like this one, or had the quality of haze it'll ooze for a rider with the right patches.'

His eyes wide. 'Would you swap some haze for a place to sleep and some roady for the night?'

'That sounds all right. I need a place to rest as well. Now tell, you seen any wild brumbies up this way?'

'There's a brumby mob passes through on the way to the caves at Warby Ranges. A couple of them trucks from the mob come through, but mostly they is on the road for tradin parts or for some folks to help em mech.'

'You ever seen a girl with em? She might of got a crippled arm, scaled up like a lizard.'

'Na, I never seen that,' he said.

I gave him his haze and then later that evening the bloke with the baldy head and red beard showed up in his half track and he was curious about what we were doing there. He had a light about him, a way of being that I'd not seen before then nor again, so I stayed and talked to him some more.

'That's a nice half track ya got. Howdya keep it runnin with diesel?' I said.

'It's a secret, mate. We know a few things, a few ways of the mountains and secret stashes of things and there's folks who still got the knowin of refinin fuel oil and machinin parts. I can do it a bit me self and I know how to fix a engine.'

I was sort of in awe of him because I didn't know nothing, only wrangling and the ways of haze. Here was someone not tied in to a system with a truck or camp or Wotcher show, he was free.

'I'm Jon Ra, what's yer name?'

'I'm called Bushy. Short for the Bushy Ranga on a count of me ruddy beard.'

'Do ya got any commerce with the brumby mob for fuel or parts or such?'

'They come through here but they don't run on no diesel that's for sure. Who knows what their program is. Sometimes they stop for fixes that they can't mech themselves with robo droans. I done some tough weld fixin on one of em just a few days back.'

'They raided a backroads shanty town right about then, lookin for parts and other truckbodies to mech. Maybe one of them was busted in the raid. They stole me sis. I'm roadin after them to get her back.'

He went all quiet then, looked away.

I said, 'Yer know somethin bout that? A girl, maybe sixteen, who's been roadin with the Brumby King?'

'Yair, I seen her. Black hair, black eyes. She's been took in by the Brumby King, I only seen just her face in the cab when I was right up close with me welder.'

Me heart flew. She was alive, at least. And Bushy'd been right up close enough to the Brumby King to see her.

'How long ago?'

'Wasn't more than four days.'

'Wherebouts?'

'Well, there's several lairs they got scattered through out. Some is in the Warby Ranges, others high up in the mountins in the snow. But where I seen the girl, it were in the gigacity.'

'But it's poisoned ground and deadly there.'

'It's not as deadly as most folks think. It's a place where all the roads end, but there's nothin there no more. The Wotcher's signal is strong there and the trucks go to get together and try to find out about themselfs in the Wotcher's image.'

'Wotcher's the cause of all me problems. If there wasn't no Wotcher I wouldn't of lost Isa.'

'Yeah well if you want to get with brumby trucks you've gotta understand a bit more bout em. They think they come from the Wotcher, and there's somethin in the Wotcher that can help them code right and make better hybrids with other trucks when they do their truckruttin.'

'Trucks can rut all they want. It's nothin to me. I just wanna find Isa and get back on to the right road.'

'Well you should check out the gigacity if ya wanna find some clues to where yer sis is at. Careful though, there's all sorts of strangeness comin outta the ground there, it's zero ground for the changes. And for the brumbies it's special ground where they gather for daisychainin and birthin babby trucks.'

'But gigacity's poisoned ground.'

'Yeah, but maybe that's not all there is to it, neither. It was the place where those who come before buried all their secrets. Look out for a place called the Lie Bury, if you wanna find out some answers.'

'How'm I gunna get there?'

'You'll find it if ya look.'

'I don't even know where to start.'

'The brumbies got their own secret passages into the gigacity. Keep on the trail.'

He left and I went back to the campfire with the other mountain folks who were high on haze and I was high on the news of Isa. I sat by the fire and thought on things while the people had a fine old time. Later on in the night there was some ugliness, some fighting, and in the morning when I clambered out of me swag pulling up me trucksuit I nearly trod right on a stiffening blue body. It was the youngster I gave the haze to. I climbed into Sinnerman and we roaded out of that place. It pulled on me soul with a sadness, though I should have been happy because I'd found someone who had seen Isa. I couldn't account for me feelings, except to say being around folks who have lost all hope of themselves breeds hopelessness. So I took my toll from them and gave what they wanted, what does that make me? I didn't want to think on it as I roaded through the mountain towards the gigacity and the Brumby King that I knew now was up ahead on this very same road. There was nothing I could do, just had to deal with the stain on the world so on I rolled with Sinnerman. It was a blessing to be back inside that cab.

Chapter 12

Coming out of the ranges there was a body twisting in the branches of a tree as we ran for the pass between the mountains and the sea of the east. Sign of the dead man's hand on the road to the gigacity and the secrets that were buried there. And the scrub was a blur of grey and green and the road was a line of black light out in front of us. The sun shined high in the sky and the far off white clouds were whispers of fine hair on the head of an old woman looking down on the earth below with grief in her yeller eyes.

We were moving fast through the last of the mountains' small feet before the flat in front of the coast, dust clouded up behind us. Truck action blipped on the screen. It came up faster and faster behind as we rolled. I tossed through the freeks looking for a tag but there was none. I thought: brumby for sure, running dark. It brought a smile to me face because it meant we were on the right track. And Sinnerman reckonised it too, there was a hearty thump in the system as the truck felt the loss of its partner and a rush of vengance flushed through the IV into me arm and pulled me tight and alert and ready for the chase. A spurt of blood and a spinning head through the link as me and Sinner both saw the shapes of the Brumby King and its Left Tenant looming in the glooming dust behind us in the viewscreen. The Brumby King, a hulking black monster of dusty dented panels and scratched paintwork, next to its Left Tenant, a white bastard with blue trim and a toothy grin in its grill. The Left Tenant was lighter and fast, it didn't carry no load and so it come up sweet and fast right behind us. The King following at a distance. I hit Sinnerman with some more juice through the link and it picked up the pace, swaying a bit on the road as I blinked the patch home to its truckstream.

Them two brumbies were testing us out, and Sinnerman was showing off as well. The Left Tenant matched speeds and they peacocked their flashy decals and painted glyphs to each other. The Left's grinning chrome grill was up in the rear viewscreen. It was proud as, kicking up a dust storm behind and coming on up beside us then, out gunning Sinnerman for sure in pure speed. Sinnerman's paintwork glowed blinding white and sharp red in the sun. The pair of them sped up and slowed down, and in the shadow of the Brumby King, they did the dance of the highway driving rig, one following the other in front, and pretty soon they wanted to take things to the next level. So with Sinnerman leading, they slowed up and pulled in to a flat spot where they could move to the rocking stage. Sinnerman circled around and faced off. The Left Tenant was ready for it though, it slotted a tasty groove in its sound system that I could feel through the link but not with me earshot, lazy bassline and rattling snare back behind the kick. The Brumby King pulled in as well and sat off a distance, listening to the trucksong and waiting. Left Tenant was vain and headstrong with its groove, it weren't going to let Sinnerman best it but it needed to keep control of itself in front of the King, it couldn't blow its whole load at once. It pumped out a thumping riddim as it skanked and rocked on its shocks in the desert sands.

After the first shots were still echoing around in me ears, Sinner blasted back with some of its own wavvy tunes and this time I felt the sound through me whole body. It was a tide rolling through me, breaking over the top of me head and rinsing me blood through with molten lava bass and a cool watery wash of reverb and soaking wet squelch in the high end. I blinked a new patch through the link, wanting to give Sinnerman a boost in this contest. I felt it shift and waver through the sound system as it found a change from four four to two four and sped things up. It was a rare treat listening to them two trucks battle on the highway, but it was gunna end in tears. There would soon come a finish to the rocking, and they'd be getting down to tin tacks.

The sounds flowed smooth through the air and trucktalk chatter in the link as Sinnerman and the Left Tenant sat head to head and tried to best each other with their sound systems and their skills. Putting on a flashy show, pulling samples from their memories and trying to call each other with the best take on a old tune or the freshest new vox that they'd found chattering in their stacks from the data mines. The battle went on and on, deep bass booming through me bones and me head ringing with the echo of high freek sound wash. All watched by the grim Brumby King. Sinnerman shook on its shocks under the onslaught and I kept it fed with patches to mod the waves of sound, learning as I went what made a good effect and saving up the knowing for it would come in handy for tweaking Sinner's rein, I was sure. The Left Tenant revved up hard and cranked the wattage. I could feel it in me guts, the whole cab was shaking, the noise was frightening, louder and louder and then it stopped and both trucks clunked in to gear and started their dance. Sinner spun its wheels in a mighty show of blue smoke blowing over the truck parking. Its eight rear weels were burning out and its tail came flicking around to match the Left Tenant's own circling movement as it started to shift its energy from sound to motion. The next phase in the battle was coming. Though they didn't like to scratch up their paint, once the dancing was done there weren't gunna be no worries about doing the business when it come to it. Sinnerman would ram its steel spike, it'd break out some of the fifty cal rounds it'd been hoarding. The Left Tenant would make its mark in its own way, with whatever weapons it had got stashed, hard pellets of bone or teeth or scavenged lead to sink in through shiny truckskin and rip at steel armour.

Sinner suddenly took off for the highway, slow at first, but gaining speed up through the gears as the Left Tenant caught on a second too late but followed it out soon enough. On the road with the glowing silver streaks of guide posts blur and the smooth flow of the tarmac under the tyres. Sinner got way out in front, forcing the Left Tenant to push itself into the red. Then it ever so gently slackened off the pace and lured in the Left Tenant, let it come in nice and close and then it hit the brakes and I watched the Left Tenant swerve and scream past and so we were then the ones up behind. I pushed a speedy patch through the link, and Sinnerman moved even faster on the tail of the brumby, zoning in on up for a ram or at least threatening some damage to the panels of that vain truck. The battle would leave its mark on both trucks, no two ways. The Left Tenant was wily though, it wasn't gunna let Sinnerman best it so easy. Right as rain it swerved off course and fishtailed away, donk screaming and dirt flying as its tyres bit the shoulder. Sinner held steady and wasn't gunna back down now. It was in its element, and it was pining and angry for its lost buddy Storm, though now the game had switched and it was back in front of the Left Tenant.

The Left Tenant had gotten the wind gauge now, and it wanted to send a message loud and clear so it licked with a tongue of fire from tanks of burning oil jelly under its bonnet, a spurt of flame set to singe Sinner's tail and melt its paintwork and its mood for battling. Sinner heaved. It was dead scared of fire, I realised just then. It squealed like a babby and swerved to the right trying to free itself from the gout of deep orange flame lit black at the edges with fuel smoke that I could see through the rear view. Sinner's fear came on through the IV link then, sickly grime that soured me stomach but it also gave Sinner a new burst and I worked the mix through the link, balancing off the panic with some new seeded patches to mech a good burst for Sinnerman.

It worked a trick, Sinner turned right around with a screeching of tyres and dust flying up behind. Black scatters of tyre fragments skittered all over the road and pebbles and gravel slid underneath as the whole creaking chasis rocked and came to stop right as the Left Tenant bore down. The Left Tenant must not have kept anything back with the fire, or else it was saving for another burst, but it held its distance and Sinner spun forwards with the sun glinting off the shiny tip of its ramming spike. The Left Tenant shied away from Sinner's showing of strength and courage, and also I guessed it didn't want to try its luck against that spike. So Sinner called the bluff and the upper hand switched as Sinner gunned its ram towards the Left Tenant's beautiful shining paintwork.

The Left Tenant was a crafty truck, it wasn't gunna let this unmarked indie get the best of it. It hit reverse full bore just as Sinner come on to it and spun the front wheels hard left, bringing its nose around and swinging its tail off the road and in to the dust and gravel. Sinner overshot and screamed its tyres and blatted air brakes in anger and frustration. The Left Tenant lifted up its twin fifties from inside the engine cowling and opened fire with a terrible roar and clatter of shattered bone and whooshing recoil. Spent cartilage casings scattered the ground like hail from dark green storm clouds and the rounds pinged into Sinner's armour and peppered holes into the painted panels. The Brumby King gloomed shadowly behind the backwash of smoke and dust.

A rush of pain and shock came on up through the dripline and I felt sick from it and the thought that maybe Sinnerman wasn't up to scratch with a wild brumby that made its living doing battle in the backroads. Sinner downed a gear and did a big loop around. It was aiming to get its own fifties into play and I heard the servo whine of their mounts as Sinner pulled back the housing covers. Still feeling sick as, I was just a passenger in this truck fight but I could help Sinnerman out with a little shot of something tasty through the link, so I lined up a nice hit of Red Leather from me list of patchfile tags that I read off from the linkmaker behind me eyes. The crackling burst of the patch shot through and Sinner's donk roared. Its gearbox screaming, it swung itself into firing position and opened up with the fifties. It wasn't being shy with the ammo, neither.

The Left Tenant had got itself into a tight place, it'd tried to get round for a better shot but now its backend was towards us and Sinner had the full of it in the gun sights and didn't hold back. The barrels started to glow deep red and tracer rounds arced across the space between them. Smell of gunsmoke and melted lube. It wasn't no sound system battling now, no more stances and dances. It was full on warfare between two beefy trucks that weren't gunna give in till the last one was standing. I started to feel like I was safe inside Sinnerman, like we were getting the upper hand. The Left Tenant was being ripped to bits, its beautiful body blistering up and peeling like paint in the sun. It seemed like it was pinned down with the awful pinging of bone bullets and teeth biting at steel plates and the blooming of silver shredded petals around the flowering bullet holes. Shell casings and bits of link skittered around. The sound was terrible. Sinnerman grunted and let out a throaty groan, throwing everything into the attack as it moved in closer for the kill.

Which seemed to be exactly what the Brumby King was after. Sinnerman drew in close by the Left Tenant, which must of been faking its fade, because now it sprung large and hulking in the viewscreen with Sinner in range of its flames. It turned them on big time. A wicked orange tongue of burning fuel and black smoke licked out from its jets that had swung around in their housings to face the enemy approaching from behind. The truckcab got hot. The viewscreen blacked over. Tyres were melting. Sinnerman hit reverse. The Left Tenant limped away backwards in the other direction while the Brumby King came on too, keeping pace. Through a little clear patch in the screen at the corner I could see Sinner's bright red paint turning black and crinkling like orange peel flaked off to bare steel under the flame sprung from the Left Tenant. I felt Sinner's scream burning through the link and into me own body like I was the one on fire. I opened me mouth but nothing come out except a dry croak. Me eyes were wired wide with the pain and the rush of adrenaline and truckjuices flushing through the system. Sinnerman wasn't holding its own no more. It turned one eighty and fled the firey burst with the Brumby King close behind and burning fuel. We managed to break free of the flames and it turned out that Sinnerman could out run the bulky King, though it didn't make much difference now we'd turned tail and run.

The road bucked underneath and the sky so high above, we felt the sun hot on our burnt metal skin and it was a delicious feeling, sucking in gulps of fresh air through the manifold and squirting fuel to feel this power inside rising up from underneath and setting me teeth on edge with its hold. Through the spike I got a blast from the truckjuice synthfac as Sinner caught more clear air in its grill, a rushing dream and the bush roadside fell into a green haze blur and I was dreaming out loud, a riot of colour and movement all around. Me eyes were wide as with the thrill of doing battle. Roading with the Brumby King's dust cloud disappearing behind, where we was gunna outrun it even though before all I'd wanted to do was catch up to it.

That was my thinking that bright morning of smokey dealings and burnt up paint, my manifolded future coming on up straight ahead but of course things are never as straight ahead as you would like them to be. There's always twists and one was waiting for me right there. Nerve toxin shook me outta my haze, the crippling pain of it shuddering through the spike into me arm. Some choking white innerference from the link that had been sent by an evil brumby truckmind to chock our shocks.

Screaming.

Sinnerman screaming too, wheels locked up, spinning outta control.

The Brumby King slotting some wicked trucking magic through the link, grinning at us through the open rear hatch as it caught up.

Dusty black paintwork and massive chunky snub nose filled up the hatch. It knew it'd gotten our number with the trump card, its one shot of system cripple fired through the link at just the right time and already working its way through Sinner and then through me.

We were goners, at speed.

Time slowed right down.

I was looking out of me eyes as if I was someone else watching on a screen.

I seen the way the sun light glinted off the tiny chips of minerals in the gravel at the side of the road and I felt the sway and shudder through Sinner's body as it tried to right itself but got it all wrong, oversteered and then we were into the roll. I couldn't believe we'd gone from so high one minute ago to this, running against the soft edges and rolling over into the scrubby dust. The noise of it was loud in me ringing ears, the smell of burning sharp in me nose. Straps pulled tight across me chest, me head snapping with the lurch.

The sun whirled around us like a golden whip and blue sky swapped with black earth till time caught up again and we came to a stop and the noise ended. Then it was just the spinning of a wheel and the creaking of steel and the ping and tick of cooling metal.

I was still strapped in all right but me head had snapped around in the jarring crash and me mouth was bleeding where I'd bit me lip. I hanged sideways down inside the cab. There was nothing from Sinner through the link. Dust blowed past outside, I could see the ground. I flipped the release on me harness. IV came out with a crusted pull of bright pain and along with it a lotta blood and some tendrils where the flesh had been grown into by the feed. I was more a part of Sinner than I realised and it shocked me how fast I'd got truck wise. I hit the deck and coughed up a lung. Already the dust and smoke were getting inside me head. I had to make a move.

I kicked out the hatch and crept outta there into the bright sunshine. I tried to stand but I couldn't. I was cold and sweating and me heart was still racing. A wave of sick rolled up from me stomach and I vomited. The blue sky above, red dusty earth under me back. I laid there a while and then it clicked what'd gone on but I couldn't even roll over again before there was a

ANDREW MACRAE

swooshing from above and a flapple flew overhead. Flight of the
death bird come to pick shreds from the corpse. The Brumby
King grumbled closer, the Left Tenant limping behind. They
knew Sinner were finished, lying on its side like that. A roll out
here could kill off a truck quicker than bullets. But I thought I
felt a burst on the link from the Brumby King as it rolled slow
past, just a flash and then gone and I didn't know what it could
mean so I put it outta me head. I was sickened with the crash
but I could still see out me eyes, though I was stricken roadside
same as Sinner. As the King passed I thought I caught a look of
a pale face framed with dark hair and dark eyes lit by a rectangle
of light from the rear viewscreen. It was just a flash and it was
gone but I knew it was her and I knew she must need me help
more than ever, kidnapped by the Brumby King.

Me sick heart quickened even more. I pulled the linkmaker
with feverish fumbling, blinking for Sinner and there were signs
of life. It was rebooting, but slow as. System crash. Damage
to the body, though it'd only rolled the once. I couldn't see no
leaks or nothing. No smoke or fire, not yet anyway. Pretty soon
there'd be roadcrew and all manner of scavengers turning up.
I couldn't even stand, let alone walk to run after Isa and the
Brumby King. Best I could do was crawl away a bit further
towards a patch of prickly pear where I could watch their tracks
disappear into the dust.

I sheltered there under wizened cactus till I got myself
together. I kept on zoning in and out and me eyes were hard

to keep open. I didn't know what was going on, me arm started aching real bad from where I'd been pulled separate from that big truckbody lying on its side in the dust by the road. We were laid low and I couldn't see no way out. Pretty soon the flapples and bigdogs would be along to ping Sinnerman's skin and I thought that'd probably be the end of my tale, too.

Chapter 13

Sinnerman was ten tons of metal and gears and self-salvaged tech out in the sun there lying on its side in the rust coloured dust. A tawny flapple sat up high on the top, creaking as it folded its wings. It screeched like an old metal hinge and I heard the ping as it pecked at metal skin. I crawled back over and tried to push on Sinner but I couldn't shift it. Even if I were hale and hearty I couldn't of shifted it. I laid down in the dirt. I was gunna need some help to make it through. Some help, and then some more. A pack of bigdog robos gathered and it reminded me of the time I sat beside me Mum after she died birthing a dead babby.

Wasn't long before Crow showed up, of course. Whenever there's misery or misfortune, there's always Crow come to pick the bones and see what he can find.

'Looks like you've hit a snag,' he said.

'Yeah, well me truck's rolled over.'

'That's a real shame.'

He eyed the wreckage and me crusted arm and reeking pale body, and his wet tongue licked dry lips.

'Carn, don't just stand there like a statue, gimme a hand tryin to right this truck,' I said.

'Mate, you know it don't work like that. I'm here to see what's of use in this wreck.'

'It's no wreck, it's me truck Sinnerman and we're gunna be back on the road before the likes of you can get yer claws in.'

'I dunno about that, boy. Youse've got some serious problems. That truck's on its side.'

He looked at me sharpish through eyes so clear they were almost white inside, and nothing shining in the black.

'I'm just gunna sit down and have a smoke,' he said.

He sat down under the shade of Sinners truck body and took out a little pipe, loaded it with ganja from a leather packet. Sparked up and blowed smoke in me face. Meanwhile Sinner was rebooted and trying to fire its engine to get things moving. Not that it would of done much good the way things were.

I looked at Crow closer. He was changed since I last saw him. Looked almost younger in some ways, not so many creases round his eyes. Same trucktyre coat, but. Same hair down to his shoulders though it were turning back from white to black. I shivered inside, it wasn't a homey feeling, being tied together with a creature like that on the roading through the country of the end times to truck knows where.

There came a rumbling on the road just then, and I seen

Crow's eyes flicker, his face fallen downcast even at the same time as me own heart raced at the prospect of another truck on the horizon. I climbed to me feet and rested one arm on Sinner's dusty under carriage and with the other I flicked me linkmaker on and scanned the freeks for the new comer. I was seasoned as a truck rider now, I'd gotten a good idea of what patches would entice an indie to stop and take a listen. I blinked a few and up popped a truck, coming fast but starting to slow at the sign of a rider on the road. Crow packed another cone and watched from the side. It was an indie coming all right, it came in to view shining in the sun like the promise of a new day. A second chance. Slowing up even further when it saw what I'd got to offer but it was wary too at the site of a freshrolled truck by the roadside.

Yeller Mackdog, pulling a trailer full of parts from the Midden Dump. Liked the sounds of what me linkmaker was making, pumped a happy tune. Sinner too sick from the rollover to make a sound. I held the linkmaker and blinked through a new patch and the truck was a bright one, it knew right away what was required. Its signal went weak then strong as the patch worked its way through its system. Even in my sickened state I was able to fix a rope from Sinners tool box and tie it high up on to the Mackdog's body. Crow just sat there the whole time, smoking up and silent now it looked like there weren't gunna be nothing to pick from the wreck after all. I spent some time scouting for sticks and wedged them in under Sinner's six wheels

ANDREW MACRAE

on the ground to give some leverage when the pull came on, so it wouldn't just slide in the dust. When it was all ready, I gave the Mackdog another little taste of the patch it wanted and it went the old heave ho. Slowly, slowly till it reached the tipping point of balance where if you find it you can do magic, that place that's there but not there. It's still even though it's moving. And then the fall and creaky crash as Sinner rocked on its shocks.

Sinner was rebooted by then and hauled back on to its wheels. It flashed its lights groggily in silent thanks to the Mackdog which was happy it'd gotten its patches for hardly any work at all and it took off down the road as I climbed into the cab once more and hooked myself into Sinnerman. Leaving Crow by the roadside, we moved along through the slow day, sunlight flowing thick like golden syrup from a can but Sinner wasn't the same truck. It was cruising with a limp, its heart wasn't in it. It was all scratched up and scarred and blackened and while I thought the new wounds made it look tough, I knew that for a proud indie it was the worst thing that could happen ever so I pushed it gently along looking to find somewhere to get fixed up. Camp after camp we roaded until two days after the crash and off track from the gigacity we came on a truckstop that had a shop there for detailing. Them indies were mad for the truckskin art that the detailers marked out on metal. Marks made by the detailers who interpreted messages they saw from the Wotcher and etched on the indies that would come from miles around for the latest bit of flash. For their part, the detailers were happy to transact for truckdream haze and Wotcher clips from the wild indies.

Pulled over and while our dust caught up with us I sat in the cab and checked the scene. There was a bloke with welding goggles pushed up on his white skull, looked like he knew what was what. Four indies crowded around him. I thought for sure he was chief truck detailer at this truckstop. Hustle bustle in the shop with detailers moving between the trucks cutting deals, lighting stencils, marking up trucks, leading them in for the enamel bin, those creatures, those amazing wild creatures made of steel and darkness and light. Just looking at them massing like that filled me with wonder. Who knew what they thought? The only way you could guess at what they wanted was by looking at their acts and most times what they did didn't make any sense at all. Who could of guessed they'd be into the tricks of the skin, hooking themselves into the linked mirror cams set up around the spraybooth that gave them three-sixties over their bodies. Blasting out fat tunes between them when the mood took. Some of the designs were unreal and many I thought were just ugly mess but the trucks themselves didn't, no way. They rolled around proud as punch. Smokestacks blarting and the smell of them, always the smell, it got me high and it got the detailers high, you could see it in their eyes, they were as hooked on the trucks as we riders were, hooked as the trucks were on them. Moving among them, making marks on the gentle metal skin, just to touch them, to feel them up close.

It's what I wanted too but I was a roader, I couldn't make no artwork, and anyway I had me own path to tread. There were always new things coming through the pipeline between the trucks and the Wotcher, like one week it would be scrollwork and lace and the next fluro lights and bright shining things and then symbols that pattern and shift as how you look on them.

I pulled out the IV feedline from me arm. It came with a sting and a pucking of flesh up around the spike. Didn't much like being disconnected but it was the only way I could negotiate and anyway I'd have to leave Sinnerman while it was getting meched. Me boots clanged on the rungs as I climbed out of the cab. Shaky feet on the ground. It felt like I was still moving on the highway with Sinnerman rumbling underneath me but really it was just me and me meatsuit now. Wobbling through the detailers I found the bloke I'd seen at the start, with the goggs on his head, and I went to him and asked, 'Can you fix me rig?'

His eyes were spaced, the grin on his mouth was wide and careless.

'What's that, mate?' he said.

'Me rig, Sinnerman. We been messed up pretty bad in a rollover.'

'Oh yeah? How'd that happen?'

'It was brumbies.'

'You know which mob?'

'I call them the Brumby King mob, run by a big black barstid that don't take no care for its appearances.'

'I know em. They don't come here for mechs, but I know em.'

'Well they ran us off the road and left us for flapple snack in the backroads. Managed to get righted, but Sinner's not feelin the best and I'm wonderin if you could fix it and make it right again, cuz we is both roadin after the mob and now we want revenge,' I said.

'Nah, mate. Not up to me. You better aks the boss.'

He pointed over to where there was a woman in overalls, round hips and pear chest. She sat quietly crosslegged and zoned out in the busy space, work happening around her but somehow also within her. Looking at her now, I couldn't work out how come I'd missed her to start with. The other detailers bowed their heads to her as they passed and the trucks were ordered in deference to her, at the centre of her own daisychain of one and everyone.

I went up to her but I was blocked by her offside, a hardbitten bloke with lead for eyes.

'What do I have to do to get me rig looked at,' I said.

'Just wait your turn, mate. There's no system or plan here except as what's laid out by the boss.'

I walked back to where Sinnerman was lowing, looking real down since the crash, all bashed and burnt, and grass and sticks caught up under the wheel arches and in between the panels.

I went back to the bloke with the goggs. It looked like it were gunna take a while so I settled in by his side as he worked. He said his name was Lam. After a while I asked, 'So waddya know of the Brumby King's mob?'

Lam's face was greased in creasemarks when he smiled his brokentooth grin. He said, 'They're causin all sorts of trubbil aroun the backroads. Our indies is all antsy coz they're feared the brumbies will slave new trucks for their mob. The Brumby King is after breedin stock, tryin to build up its follerin.'

'Any idea where they is holed up?'

'Na, mate, they come and go. I think they got a few diffrint hidey holes about the place. I heard one of them is in the Warby Ranges — they got a cave there — but they shift round so much its hard to say and they is always on the move, carryin everythin they they need and raidin whatever else. I also seen in the gigacity, searchin in the ruins for signs of the Wotcher's passin.'

'They'd stop for foragin fuel sometime, but.'

'Dunno, maybe not. I heard the black one runs nuke, but thats just rumour.' He paused then said, 'Mate, it's not gunna be a easy wrangle.'

'I don't think so neither. The Brumby King took somethin of mine and I want to get it back, thats all.'

He was right, it was a few days before the patternings of trucks around the boss fell into place and Sinnerman could get seen to. Meantime I hung around with the detailers, trading yarns and writing me thoughts down in me typewriter. I saved them together where all the trancecrypts of Smoov's rants were kept, clipped up in the lid of the HERMES case. I thought maybe I were getting the beginnings of a trancecryption of me own, and if not I were at least getting things straight in me head.

The first night in the truckstop I watched as the detailers gathered after darkness come down. It was time for the Wotcher's passing and the boss had got her decks together and the detailers and their camp followers that hung on like skinny yeller dogs pushed in closer to the show. Behind the screen Sheila tuned in with the Wotcher like a showman would, except instead of making meanings with truckshows, what she pulled out were pictures from the Wotcher's feed. Different designs came out of the staticky waves, spirals and shapes, hard blocks or soft edges. Pictures of different trucks through the ages, trucks from the past time that the Wotcher beamed down. I realised they were the markings that were gunna be etched onto the trucks they were working on.

Next day I walked through the camp watching the detailers and seeing how the trucks come in from the backroads looking for the patterns from the night before. Thinking on how the trucks loved that stuff from the Wotcher, it was like they were looking to find their own image in the static that got beamed down from on high each night. Those indies looked to the Wotcher for answers just like the showmans and the camps did, except for the trucks there was something real at stake. Maybe they thought the Wotcher could give them some secret codes in mechin their new hybrid forms, like maybe the Wotcher had the knowing of their first codes from before things went all bad with the gigacity system. Maybe they needed the codes to be everything that they wanted to be, not having to mech new parts all the time from herding up spare trucks but something that could heal itself like a wound would scar up, not break down.

When the sun got too hot I went off down the gully to wash me own wounds and took some haze like I was growing accustomed to it. The sky was dotted with shapes hanging in the air and riding the breeze. At first I thought they were some new kind of flapple but then I seen they were tethered to the ground and rode on strings by kids that were floating them up there in the sky. They made an eerie sound like frogs or angered insects as the wind shook through their cloth feathers. I ate off of a grill the camp followers set up under a blue tarp beside a trickling creek and watched the kids float their flying things. Some of the flyers were real skilled, could make the things on strings do dips and loops and fight against each other. As well as the detailers there was another cult there sharing the camp, a goannaman looking after a big lizard that was all painted up with signs and symbols. Seemed that everyone had their own kind of creature outside of themselves that was gunna bind them together into a whole. I could tell the goannaman were well thought of in the truckstop, he got the best cuts off the grill. His goanna crunched up the bones and maybe it were how they kept out the flapples and robodroans, by having the goannaman around to clean up all the carrion. There wasn't nothing left there for them to scrounge. It also made me feel safe from Crow too even though I'd only seen him a few days ago. Where there were too many scavengers already, Crow wasn't likely to show up.

Another night came on down again and I started to get itchy to be roadin after Isa. I'd gotten some good leads on the brumby mob and wanted to get to the gigacity to start the search there. Sinnerman was being worked on but wasn't ready yet. But there was no hurrying along the detailers. They had their own time marked out, and it wasn't set by the rising and falling of the sun. They'd go on for three solid days on a job and then crash and sleep right through for a day. It was set by the timing and motion of the Wotcher, but also it come down to what was being broadcast in the trancemission. If there wasn't anything they could use in there, they'd just get tanked up some more and fight with each other round the fireplace. All the while that goanna-man's reptile monster crunched on bones. It got me nerves jangled and I was getting itchy for Sinnerman's IV again too. I sneaked up inside Sinnerman's cab and loaded up, even though it wasn't ridgey didge to do it while there wasn't no roading happening. It kept me going and I kept Sinner going with a splay of new patches I'd been working on, and I could feel we was both rebuilding our strengths from the battle with the Left Tenant, and who knew what else was coming round the bend for us.

Two days later the boss got done with Sinnerman and Lam came out and he shook me hand and said, 'Where you headed now?'

'Gunna road towards the gigacity I reckon.'

'Fair enuff. The Wotcher's signal's strong there. There's a place called the Lie Bury where them from the past times is buried all the lies, it's somewhere near the centre of where the Wotcher's freek can be tuned. Keep yer eyes out for it.'

I shook his hand.

'Hooroo,' I said.

I turned and walked to Sinner's fresh mint truck skin glistening with sparkling new glyphs, still red and white and with a western look but new designs and new tweaks to its running gear. I almost didn't wanna dusty up its steps with me boots as I swung up in to the cab. Slotted home the spike and Sinner gunned up again and the flow of the haze met me own blood flowing pounding into me heart and the machine of me dreams. Slowly we roaded back out into the bright sunlight, so blinding and strange after that dark shed of truck magic and the long campfire nights. The gigacity loomed large on the horizon ahead.

Chapter 14

Sinner was feeling more of its usual self with the road shaking and shuddering underneath its rolling wheels riding on the coast road. It wasn't more than a day before we could see the steel skeletons of towers looming ahead on the viewscreen. As we came closer, I saw more and more flapples flying like flies around the bodies of dead trucks, crushed fliers and scattered robos and telly presents droans in the broken lands. Bodies of roadkilled roos and camels and people too, black as engine oil from a busted sump. Smoke rising up from the stripped chassis bodies. Bricks and blocks and chunks of concrete, bits of bitumen and all the rubble from the buildings of lost times when the gigacity was towers of glass and thin pollymer plastic glittering in the sun like a million streams of waterfalling stars, living machines of glass and smart thinfilm building minds talking and transacting in a brilliant system built of light stretched over steel bones. That's the picture I had of it in me mind from when Isa told me that time of the stories from the past and I seen them overlaid on the earth outside the window and it was a shadow that stained the ground and rose up like wisps of smoke behind me eyes, like the dream coursing through me system with the black liquor that leaked through the IV from Sinnerman's alkaloid synthfac. The land outside the cab flowed past like a smooth surface, I couldn't penetrate beneath. And maybe there's nothing beneath at all, maybe the surface is all there is but still you gotta try to break through. So we rolled over the skin, looking for a way in.

The gigacity beckoned up ahead and the shadows of that place made me shudder and I understood how come folks never went there no more. Shimmering like a lost world. The screen seemed a part of me. No highlights anymore. Nothing, just the flow, just the jets that moved me along through the deep water of a truckbound life, losing the use of me limbs, me memories all jumbled up out of order like a cloud of locusts flying over the road. Still there was a pattern and everything I saw was filtered through the screen. Me and Sinnerman was a system, but which one was the host and which the parasite? I was living on haze and rolling through the backroads in the machine, but Sinner was living off me patches as well, living off me code wrangling as I led it up to be broken on the highway and when we found Isa, it would be in a slaughterhouse of brumby trucks. All the handsome trucks and their running lights shining bright in the night behind me eyes. It was all gunna catch up with us sometime, we were running ahead of a foamy wave and soon it would break us but I pushed them thoughts away and kept on going.

I was deep in that connection and it was scary and wonderful too, a new page cranked into the typewriter. I'd never been so close to another creature in me whole life. Even Isa done nothing but push me away. And now I had this connection what had got me in its hooks, it'd got me in its spiked arm. Its IV and its hazy visions. This creature that I didn't even know till just a few days ago was now me whole life, and yet me life was not a whole and we were riding together into the gigacity looking for Isa, my lost sister my lost lover my lost half. Hid below the surface all you find is more surfaces.

We drove in through the outskirts. Cinderblock boxes and broken corners piled with rubble. Rubble piled on troubles. No one around, it was a ghost town left for dead by those who lived there and cursed ground for us who come later. We kept on, though it were slow going. The road hadn't been kept through passage. The robo roadcrew builders that kept the backroads on their own programs weren't in sight of the gigacity. And in the backroads at least the tracks though rutted and ridged was kept opened from so much traffic passing through. My whole life passing through, one stop to the next.

The houses where once there was people were all long since looted and burnt. Frames pulled apart for fuel, fire blackened fronts stained with sooty smoke. I rode high up in the rider's cab, feeling the growing wonderment of that place and all its glass ghosts were grown on me like creepers on a tree, slowing me down on the road and all the stories I'd heard of the gigacity danced in me head. I couldn't keep them separate from what I saw in front of me eyes. The stories infected the daylit towers of tangled steel like a virus so they seemed to glow in the afternoon sunshine and called out to me with the voices of all those whose footsteps and trucktracks had gone before in the world and all them who were dead and left to rot out in that place of poisoned ground and slinking snakes moving shapes in the corners of me eyes. I saw it and I didn't see both at the same time. I knew it was in me mind, I knew it was the stories, I knew it was both what I seen and not seen and all at the same time. Most of all I knew then why there was so many stories of the gigacity and why it wasn't a place to be visiting or for living in them ruins long since left for leavings good and proper.

On and along we went, slow and careful forging a path through the shattered wreckage. It took a while to see it but the city was being taken back by rioting life. Roots growed up through everything, tangled creeping greenery clawing at the red brick. Lizards and slithering creatures scrubbled out of the way as we crawled through. Either side the buildings loomed and got thicker and taller towards the centre. Ahead a steel canyon wall above a river of glittering glass shards beneath.

We come to a place of dead ends. Five ways intersecting. The buildings here were seamless towers, their tech all bound up and sealed behind grim black surface. I had a flash it could be just like Isa said, the buildings was standing ready and waiting for the right codes to get started in working again and restoring the past system. We made our way through broken laneways and busted concrete. Burn scars wherever I looked. I felt like I'd been there before, in a dream. Shiver of craving for the missing haze flow became a new syntax written in me blood by machines not built by human hands.

Time's ticking, time sticking. Time didn't flow straight forwards like most people were happy to think. You could slip down inside of it, you could feel its texture. It's grainy, not smooth. It comes out in lumps and clumps around certain things that you keep coming back to in your memory. If all time was the same, how come there's some moments that stick out from others, some faster, some slower? Then there's them other times when you look up from what you've been doing and you see it's near dark and you'd not realised the day passing. Cruising the gigacity street sweating out haze visions from me skin, I was remembering and *re*membering, bringing memories back to me mind, like a feeling that breaks through from the other place, from a different place down where the river bends by the creek side in the wet season and the daylight stretched to its end and I was there with Isa and the creatures that lived in the rocks and the stone and a slinky snake slithering in the muggy sunshine. We were all lost in time, the things we see in front of our eyes, in front of our −I−s, is what takes up most of the brain but if you can shut them out for a time, the memories start coming up, the things that happened and maybe they didn't even happen but on some level you know they did. Some level, some time, some Wotcher seeded those signs in your head. But try to grasp it and it's already gone, like a slinky snake into a crack in the rocks.

Through the viewscreen I seen grooves in stone steps on the gigacity pathway. There was something about the place that made me mind move. The stairs were sagging like the grooves in Smoov's linkmaker where me greasy fingers thumbed the shiny metal clean. I thought about all the trudging feet that had made those grooves over so much spans of time and maybe it don't matter what I thought or typewrited anyways, it was all gunna be dust soon enough. There wouldn't be no one left who could read it, no one to decode these writings. But then maybe it's like the grooves in them steps, someone would see the passing from the bits that *aren't* there in this place where roads came to die. The words twist in on themselves and there's no way in or out in that blasted landscape of red rock and smooth brown stone in the dried up creek beds of dry city streets that have never flowed for a hundred years or more. It's just deadly death and danger to anyone passing by. A broken neck and stolen boots. Let me die in trucktyre shoes tied up with twine so they'll know I died standing up.

Chapter 15

The day bled into moonfaze in the gigacity where the wreckage from the time before piled up on the underside of overpasses by the broken banks of the river. Stacks of rusted shipping cans piled like the broken toys of a babby mountain sprung loose from its roots. A plastic tide of black water flecked with styrofoam. I rolled in Sinnerman along the busted pathway. I'd not seen a sign of anybody at all since I been in the city, and there were reasons for it. Looking down to the side, there was movement down there in the rubble. Staring closer and I seen it was a slinky snake, segments of its body like a earthworm and a red eye light lit for its hunting of warmth and skin and fur to feed on. And then the more I looked, the more of them I seen, squirming in the corners of me eyes. There wasn't just one, there was a hundred. Long as I were inside of the truck I were safe, so we set to roaming, rolling on the road that criss crossed the river and the water, broken down parts of freeway shattered on the ground, picking our way through the mess looking for signs of brumby life.

The night blur of cruising the gigacity. The roads twisted around each other and led back to the same place. Down inside a tunnel and then back on up the other side, wrecked trucks lit under lights. Some roads were broken and some weren't, so we felt our way through there, looking out brumby tracks but there was none. Over and under it all, the stench of death and smoke rising from the ruins but it weren't so bad as some places I been. Sinnerman was antsy for the next to point the way but I kept it held tight. There had to be a way out of the swirling ruins and scavenged meats from the trickery of the rubble that moves according to the light that falls on it. If I could get to the place where that truckdetailer told me the Wotcher's signal could be tuned louder and clearer. Through the night I sat in the cab and I searched for the connections that would unlock the meaning in it all. Wrote down what happened and what I seen on me typewriter and rifled Smoov's notes just trying to come to some understanding of the world rolling them streets overgrowed with greenery and creepers. Broken signs and light rail lines stretched on a long road that ran through a canyon of twisted steel.

Some force drawed me onwards to Isa, pulled me along through the streets as daylight started to shine between the towers and the water rising up through buildings that stuck out of the ground like rotted teeth from a black gum. River broke the bank and flooded out all over the place, out of where it would be its own self. I spent the next day searching through burnt out cars and the remains of them who was gone from the world now. There wasn't much left, the place was picked clean like white bones bleached in the sun. And yet there was plenty still in the places in between. And all the blue tarps in the world couldn't keep off that rain that blowed from the south and the afternoon sky hung low and dark and the buildings sailed like downside up ships in a black and stormy sea.

We came to a broken door in a wall. It opened on to a garden secret and lush and green, I'd never seen nothing like it, it were a pair of dice there in the ruins beset on all sides by dust and crumbling stone chaos. I pulled at the IV in me arm but it were clawed so deep it had become stuck. I saw inside the gap in the wall to that place, it were so green. There were many different kinds of plants, fronds and spines and leaves, not like anything else in the backroads of dried up spinifex and scrubby brown shrubs. I wanted to check it out so I pulled harder and finally the IV come out with a well of blood that I staunched with me sleeve. I hobbled Sinner with linkmade patch to keep it still while I were gone, though neither of us fancied lingering long in that place crawling with poisoned life and there in the corner of me eye a brumby skitter skated.

I climbed down, me legs was none too good, but something in the garden pulled me on. From the outside, the space inside didn't seem big enough to hold all that wild raging riot of life overgrowing rubble of the city. There was a spiral pathway that led to the centre and as I passed through, brushing leaves and crunching gravel through the smell of damp and mouldy forest, I wish I knowed all the names of the plants. I wondered if there was anyone left who knowed the names of all them trees and whether you could brew their barks for a tonic and stuff like that. It got me thinking, but. That garden were real well tended. The whole place, although it was quiet, although it was wild, there was a method to it. It'd been planned and it'd been kept. It was a place of peace and lightness. It come to me then that the differents between a garden and a forest were that a garden had a system and someone or something to arrange it and look after it and pull out the weeds. Also a garden were *for* someone and a forest was just for itself, and I wondered who the garden was for in that lonely place where only the wind spoke through the walls. Right at the center of the garden I found a hole with a doorway. Yanked it open and inside was darkness and beckoning cool from the heat of the day.

I didn't know what was inside the garden, nor who could of been looking after it, nor why, but I went on in through the door out of the sun shine and into shadows of a musty room. That brumby skitter scrabbling in the stones somewhere. The hisspering sound of fans and a soft flow of air told there was still the remains of sun harvested power and the ticking turbines from the roof trickling their electricity into the ruined building's circuits. Me eyes got used to the darkness inside. In on down and there was a well worned pathway in the dust. Signs of life there, not just from machines and animals neither. I stood there waiting, listening, me breath coming and going through me throat. Particules of light danced on the insides of me eyes in the dark.

I felt me way forwards in the gloom and slowly I could see there were lights coming from glowing strips in the walls. It wasn't much but it was enough. I come down the steps into a open space where the stair cases were twined around a central shaft and so I climbed, driven by curiosity, being pulled up by something that I couldn't explain and I thought all of a sudden: What if there was a rider slotting patches in me own brain? What would such a creature look like? Would it see out of me eyes like view screens in a truck cab?

At the top of the stairs the space opened out to a massive round room, spokes drawing inwards to a centre platform. Muddy light came in from windows at the top of a dome ceiling. The sound were hushed inside, I could hear the currents moving in the air filling up a space that stetched as I stretched me neck up to the top, past the balconies jammed with shelving and bound books fallen to the floor in piles of tumbled pages yellered and eaten up with age. It was the Lie Bury. I shuffled through the dust, feeling the power of that space, it were a holy place I could tell. I almost were holding me breath and a creepy feeling crawled up the hairs of me back as I walked up to the centrepiece with five sides and I felt like there were someone watching me.

Inside a black hole stretched on downwards into the dark. It were a entry hatch fetched up by something on a long line of robo arm and track what pulled up from beneath. Down in there a whirring sound were happening and a swift grind; there was light coming up from down in there too. So down I went, on down in to the black towards the light. Me beard was scraggy from no washing. I was the heatsink on an overclocked donk, a patchfile change log, a speck of grease spat from the hot frying pan ready to sizzle. The show reel unwinding in me head as I lurched in towards where we were coming up on the centre of things, feeling the weight of history and the wording of the past.

I went up closer and saw the bristling centipede of a hundred legs crawling and the voice of a crow cawing and the scraping of the weight of me own body over the rusted metal of the hatchway. Down into the well, where I knew the end was waiting. The shaft ended and opened out onto a wide-open space splayed with patterns of light and shadow. A robo arm whirled backwards and forwards, there were stacks and stacks of all them books and papers. The arm was being fed by what were left of the electricity trickling trickery from the roof. It whined on its tracks, hissing as it shuffled the books in the stacks. I walked towards it, seeing what it was doing. It danced around in the hole, ordering the books in some way, coding the spines of them all what were black in one part and all what were red in another. Then it did them again. Standing back in the dim light I could see there were shapes coming out from the patterns and shifting into forms that I could reckonise. This was the place where all the lies come to be buried.

A pattern formed up in the black against the red, an image of a crow, wings spread. I just stood there as the shape of black wings flicked in to being by that spinning arm what started to move faster as it got closer towards the end and then it stopped. There was no sound but the dust falling. I stared at the shape of the crow there for the longest time. The black stain shaped like wings that didn't go away when I closed me eyes. Crow was always there, waiting for me, singing me to do his work.

Watching the arm doing its work, I seen there wasn't no easy way to ask the past what it was about. There wasn't no way of knowing what it was like back then. Their systems were a mystery, and who knew what they made of, the work on the shoulders of the world that come before even them?

I could ask the Lie Bury of books to fetch its arm and call one up for me, but I'd got Buckley's of making any sense out of it. All I could do would be guessing.

Inside that crow that were made by machine and etched behind me eyes, I seen a blank space. A missing book. The arm kept trying to reach for it, but there was nothing there so it had to work around the hole like a tongue on a broken tooth. I kneeled down on the ground and saw the footprints in the dust, too, and a long hair what weren't from any human. It shook me out of a trance. Even in this place where the signal was strong from the Wotcher, it was still all messed up out of place, but someone had taken that book from the Lie Bury. It made me think. There were someone who had come before, and I realised Isa's dreams of reseeding the gigacities was as lost as the dust fallen to the floor. The only hope in the world would not come from the patterns of the old. It were there, out east, where the Warby Ranges called like a crow.

Chapter 16

Out in the sun it was real bright and hot. Me eyes were dazed. I picked me way back through the ruins to where I'd hobbled Sinnerman by linkmade rope and patch, tethered under a tree what had growed into the wall with its roots all twisting through the bricks and cracks. Popped the hatch and climbed back into the rider's cab with Sinnerman. The homey smell of it hit and I felt the rumbling of power and light as Sinner fired up and I slotted the IV. Through the link were a mix of colour and sound joined with me blood. It came on hard. I was jonesing for the feed and Sinner itched to be on the prowl again and for me it was good to be back teamed with that massive truck. The connexion growed between us and I felt the particules from Sinners synth mod feed coming through the IV again and me own flesh closing around the spike. Using just me mind I could mod the patches through the link now. They were like coloured lines of light behind me eyes and I could put em together now so that Sinnerman would feel what I wanted to do and it would do it.

Out from all them slinky snakes, just a hankering then for an open road and some space around me and the image of Isa and how we could be together. Trick of the light threw sunflash of bright truckskin in a space between the buildings. Tantalising, a glimpse of brumby headed north. I fed Sinner some files and it swung around and we rolled back up to the overpass but there wasn't nothing there except a brumby skitter shooting off towards the Warby Ranges green and looming in the north and I knew then that was where I needed to road and the doubts fell off like dust in our tracks.

So I turned me mind to the Warby Ranges and we started grinding through the broken streets, heading for the north of the gigacity towards the mountains. In the distance I could see the foothills out of the viewscreen. It wasn't that far by crow flight, and it had to be the same place I'd been told about by Bushy in the western ranges and so off we went. It was like the same trip we came in on, but in reverse. The centre was glittering buildings and canyons of steel, ash and broken glass and streets blocked with rubbish and rubble piled on piles of busted brick and shattered roadway. Downed poles and wires snaking out from under them, hissing in the ill wind that blowed through the empty roads. Moving outwards we came in to thinning buildings, shorter and further apart from each other. Road still choked by lots of rubble, it was slow going to get to where it would be even more slow going when we hit the mountains. Further and furtherer out we rolled into the dense packed burbs with green creepers growing all through the buildings, blocked out and broken down petrol stations and truckstops and the crumbling walls of concrete malls a thick crust on the ground and all around. It was getting dark now and I wanted to be out of there quick smart but there was no speeding up, any mistake there and we would be stuffed. Who knew what creatures lived in those ruins that only came out at night. I'd heard many tales and I didn't want to see for me own eyes. Just being there was enough, where the peeling paint on the walls of the warped houses and the grain silos cracked and crumbled next to where the bodies of railway carriages laid spilling all their secrets of hydraulics and wiring into the earth and the slinky snakes that darted underneath and around glistening in the light from the setting sun.

Pretty soon we were down the gears through that long slow climb being pulled towards the lair of the Brumby King so high in the mountains in the dark. Sinner put on its running lights and lit up the night with greens and blues of sparkling colour that was reflected back from the trees and rocks and the black surface of the road. The way was narrow but good, recent signs of passing vehicles. We were on the right trail all right. All night running under lights. My control with Sinnerman was ingrown now, we could innerface, there wasn't much gap between thought and movement. Sometimes when I just let go I could feel it in the trancemission. I opened me mind and Sinnerman opened the throttle, engines gunning, exhaust pumping, heart beat pounding and the whine of the whirling diff. The road lies where time is tied to a place, and round and round the mountainside it unwound like a watchspring. I wanted it to go on forever, sucked into the vortex of runninglight reflection smeared in the viewscreen, but I had to face down me own fears because the Brumby King was up ahead and that was the key to finding Isa, even if she couldn't be found I had to try.

Night passed on into daytime grey and a gentle rain fell. I popped the hatch and the cool fresh air blowed in, pushed past the stink of the feed link and me crusted reeking body with its aching bones and tight gristle. Walking around in the gigacity made me realise how weak I'd got, even just from the time I'd been hooked in with Sinnerman. The thought wafted that I had to keep in shape, had to get out of the cab more and on me own two legs if I was gunna stand any sort of chance in the end, but I pushed it away because it was too easy just to roll. Best not get too far in front of yourself, you might trip and I couldn't see as how any action with the Brumby King would be faced any different to how I was rolling now with big Sinnerman at me back. Up and up into the mountains we rode. The air was getting cooler all the time, wafts of forest smell came through the hatch and the babbling warble of magpies and the bright cold lash of a whipbird. The road sighed past the viewscreen ahead round long slow curves and tight deep bends with treegreens on both sides and a long drop down off to the right into ferny gullies and misty creek beds gurgling with mossy water. Track rutted and tough but passable. Each new turn brought us closer to the lair. I could feel it coming up from inside. We were deep in the Warby Ranges now, going up slow and even slower down muddy hillslide, mud patterning up outside on Sinner's newly painted body, and it wasn't so happy that was happening but there wasn't no other way. Them hills were sitting on the centre of all the highway action, they were working in towards the gigacity on one side and the coast on the other, then past that, the dusty backroads off in the westerling. Definite signs of brumby tweeks on the trucking freek. Caught up in the breath of cold crisp air but it couldn't go on forever.

We came up near a curve in the road and there were two trucks blocking the way, two brumbies that I'd seen before. The Left Tenant and its pal, a brumby pink and grey writhing with black patterned glyphs, and behind them a bit another truck lurked. I tried to get Sinner to slam into reverse and fishtail out of there but there was nothing.

I'd got so used to the new level of innerface that it caught me off guard when Sinnerman kept rolling on. I didn't want to close too early. I struggled with all my will power but I couldn't do it.

Something was up, a different tone coming through the innerface with Sinner, and I started to track the brumbies' freek to see if I could pickup stray chitchatter but Sinnerman weren't having it, I couldn't get no signal out nor in. And then there was a new wave through the feed, some kind of haze I'd not felt before it hit, it given me a dirty grimy feeling and I zoned in and out.

Woozy head as Sinner roaded closer to where the brumbies was stood and behind them a little bit was a third truck which I knew then was Sinnerman's partner Storm, purple and yeller painted patternings I'd seen right back during the raid on the camp when I lost Isa.

'What you doin to me Sinner?' I said, even though they were airbreathed words that Sinnerman couldn't understand.

Sinner seemed to hear or at least it felt me anger in the mix of our blood and truckjuice joined together in song through the IV. There was a shudder, its last feelings of kinship towards me and then it just powered on through. It was as determined to get to Storm as I were to Isa and the sight of its lost partner so close given it a extra boost.

Time was short we were almost up on them and it was getting clearer to me what was going on, another wave of that woozy haze hit me and I knowed I had to pull the IV feed out of me arm and split from the truckcab. Even though me whole body was screaming for me to stay in, I yanked that feedline. It didn't come all the way out, it was growed in to me almost down to the bone. I could see the runners where Sinner's own metal parts had been eating into me flesh, we were both part of the same system now. Pain bit through the haze. I kept pulling with blood-slick hands and popped me harness, tore me trucksuit, pushed through nervefired agony. Me linkmaker was hot with messages firing between Sinner and the brumbies and also Storm was piping up now and pushing forwards to be closer to Sinnerman.

I realised then why the Left Tenant didn't finish us off in the backroads. It wanted to draw us up into the mountains and then it would offer Sinner a swap — give me over for Storm. And what they wanted with me wasn't certain but the brumbies knew we was on their trail since Midden Dump at least and all I could think of was the Brumby King wanted to take me alive for some reason, and well I wasn't ready to go along on them terms. Sinnerman be damned. It'd got what it wanted now, got closer to Storm.

I sprung the latch and swung the hatch and out of the cab with me tote and the typewriter. The IV came free then I was alone again in me soft body and broken and rolling at the side of the road as another two brumbies closed off behind and Sinnerman stopped at last and waited with its new brumby mates. There were plenty of messages flying on the link too fast for me to make sense and even if I could I doubt I would of known what them trucks were saying to each other.

Sinnerman just wanted to be close to Storm but the Left Tenant screamed forwards towards where I was crouched roadside. It wanted to take me for sure and I wasn't gunna get took. The other brumby though, I saw it in back, swinging round to corner Sinnerman even as I was turning to get off the track and into the bush where they couldn't follow. The Left Tenant come at me hard as it could but it wasn't enough. I was already gone over the lip. A tongue of flame shot out and singed me hind as I rolled off into a damp gully and it didn't do much other than speed me away.

ANDREW MACRAE

And as I tumbled down the mountain crashing through ferns and trees, me thoughts were bitter on how I'd been sold out by me own fucken truck.

Chapter 17

Rolled down the mountain like a stone, clutching the typewriter and me tote. Scrabbling through the scrub, legs not working proper, me arm a bloody mess, whole body screaming for the haze. I'd been part of Sinnerman for so long I was lost inside me own self, withdrawed and sick but crashing through the bush as I pushed me way down the mountain away from the brumbies and whatever their plans were for me. I didn't spare much of a thought for if Sinnerman would be feeling the pain of being apart as well, with no more patchfire wonderment from me linkmaker. I pulled the linkmaker out of me tote right then and tried to see what else was around on the mountain but the freeks were dead so down down down I rolled.

I came to rest besides a creek and drunk deep from the cool stream. I scarpered in to a little space with ferns all around and a place for me to lie till the blood crusted and the pain wore itself out. I had some roady that I ate and some roots dug from the ground and I laid there for a time. Now and again I would go to the stream for a drink and then lay back down. Night time come on and passed and daylight shone and I knew I had to keep moving so I pulled myself together and tried to stand on me dodgy legs. They were wobbly and the way was slow going but I kept on heading down. There was a path through the brush and I didn't like to think about what made it nor where it went but I needed to stay clear from the brumby lair till I could work out what to do. I'd mount another stand on that mountain side but for now I had to get myself right, wean myself off of the haze staggers.

I hit the canyon floor and in me haze crazed dreamings I looked up at the rock walls stretched up on all sides by forces that wrenched them from the earth. There's creatures that live in the rocks, they move faster than lightning and flit into cracks and crannies. Then there's creatures that is made *of* rocks. They take one hundred thousand years to make a thought, a million to say a word and when they speak a whole sentence, it's like a crack in the sky, it's like the earth is come up outta the ground and you can see the stripes of all its different colours and patternings of ages. High up in the face of the cliff I saw the features of a stone man with a stone face made of big chunks of the canyon wall. His massy stone hands clutched at thick stone bones. Weeping eyes and a line for a mouth, heavy forehead and little ears even. He was falling forever through time, fallen away from his one true love who was up on the other side of the canyon in the cleft behind me.

I seen as how they had come apart, like me and Isa come apart, by the course of time running through and splitting up the ground underneath. Some kind of cataclysm of the earth ripped two sides of the canyon one from another, two things what used to be one. That stone man was clutching at nothing. It'd taken thousands of years to happen but when the thunder come, it split the ground and tore the stone man from his cold lover and when the sky cries the rain wets his face with tears. I camped the night in that place. It was eerie quiet just the sound of the river that run through the canyon and the face of the stone man with his silent grief, only you could hear the sound of it underneath. It was one of those words that takes a million years to speak.

All next day I bashed through the scrub along the canyon floor beside the river. There was a track there, it hadn't been used for ages, there were no recent passings. So it was through downed trees and thick bush but I followed the path thinking it'd come out somewhere near a track and I could get myself another ride. I was weak and hungered when the canyon walls opened up to a green valley and I come to a shed built in the valley beside the river. I smashed the padlock to bits with a rock to see what was inside. There was a stove in there but I didn't wanna light no fire. There were signs that someone used that place sometimes, maybe as a way station on the trek through the canyon, jars of tomatoes and onions in vinager and peppers and pumpkins and zackeenies sealed away from the air in the locker and dry goods on the shelf that weren't got at by rats and animals. I made myself a home. I had a big feed and rolled out to sleep on the hard wooden bunk and nothing bothered me dreams, it was black and blissful peace for a while.

Woke up the next day forgetting where I was and whose skin I was sposed to be in. It was a odd feeling slowly remembering and realising the past was all gone now, all smashed up and bashed to bits and all I got left were this wreckage. I had to make the best fist of it though, I still burned to see Isa again and knowing as how the Brumby King put a bounty on my head for Sinnerman got me burnt up too. The burning didn't pass but I needed to fix myself right so I laid up in the valley, carrying water up to the shed from the river and then when I felt better I chopped some woods and started having a fire. Me arm healed up slow. I swum in the river and day by day I washed myself clean of the haze and the road. Jerked off to the memories of Isa in me head and made snares like Smoov taught and caught rabbits and trapped bright fish in the river.

As me strength came back I started wandering further and further out, through the hills around. I never seen another soul while I was there. It was so peaceful I didn't understand how come there was no one else around. Maybe it was cut off by the canyon and the mountains all around. The land was bountiful, but how come there wasn't no one there living off of it? The only thing I could think of was brumbies and the pull they had. So I laid low and healed myself and wandered the valleys around the mountain searching for clues and signs and a way up the summit to where I would find Isa at last.

Chapter 18

On one of me wanderings I found a path through the forest and an opening on to a bald topped mountain what had been laid bare by giant machines from the past times. The hilltop was gouged by monsters' teeth that ripped the earth up in strips of different colours. Though the bush was thick on all sides and growing back to reclaim its share of the land it was like the ground were poisoned. Nothing growed on them walls that stretched up and up in layers and steps torn in strips from the mountain. Guts of the earth vomited up and scratched bare by machines the size of what I couldn't even figure in me mind. There was one still there, a massive bucket could of held four shipping cans and its rotted metal teeth each bigger than a truckcab. Huge tracks like a dozer, three times taller than me. As I got close I could see there was no sign of use nor movement in them rusted and broken parts, just the steel frame gnawed at by flapples and feral bigdogs but too big to be busted into pieces. It was an awesome sight to see something so big and the size of the works that them what came before must of been doing. And what could be so precious in the ground? They must of been digging for some kind of secrets, something what we would never understand except with help from the Wotcher if it could be made to make sense.

I climbed in to the depths of the blasted mountain top and down in it off to one side there was a camp all ringed in wire link fence what'd fallen down and there was buildings and sheds looted and open to the weather. Walking through the wreckage of all what had gone from the past times struck a sad feeling in the silence of that place. All the power in their hands and all they done were dug big holes in the ground and rip the guts outta the world. It was a big place, they must of been mining for some serious data and some deep knowing inside that place. And on top of the sadness I realised there might still be power in the ground there yet, and if I could get it to tell its secret maybe I could find out some more about what them brumby trucks were up to. The camp was stripped bare of tools and anything useful by flappling scavengers and trucks looking for parts to repair themselves. But I wasn't looking for use or repair, I was looking for answers and a way to find out how I could make my final move to get Isa outta the clutches of the brumby mob. Maybe there was something left behind that could tell a story of brumby trucks and the way things come to this.

Crossed through over the rusted fence rattling at my passing and I walked into the camp. The Warby mountains in the near distance swallered up the sky. The sun sank behind and the valley was in shadow though there were still hours of daylight left. Hulking wrecks of machines and rusted crumbling metal gave off a nasty oily smell of tears and charcoal mixed with soil. Shipping cans with their doors swinging on broken hinges showed their rotted wooden floors to the afternoon air. Caravans and porta buildings with wilting walls and gaping windows spread their legs and let the rot have its way with them. I headed towards a shed that seemed less broken down than the others. The door opened with a groan and I come inside. In the corner there was a scarbling and a shuffling and on the outside of me vision I seen a scuttling manshape shifting from a beam of sunlight into the darkness. Me heart beat faster, it was the first human form I'd seen for days. If it was running, maybe it was more scared of me than I were of it. I called out. I was feeling bold or maybe just missing talking with another.

'Who's there?'

The silence was eery and strange. The metal of the shed pinged as it cooled from the passing of the sun. Then a feeling took hold of the back of me neck with a cold hand and I backed outta there and walked away without turning.

Back in me valley shack that night, but I couldn't get the mine camp out of me thoughts. It pulled me back the next day, I come in to the camp site and straight away I seen a path what must of gone down to the creek. Further down the pathway there was signs of fresh passing, boot marks and broken ferns so I followed along. It wasn't too rough going and a riot of green all around rushing to claim back the land. Worked me way round a stone bluff and then there in the forest beside the creek was the downed body of a massive robo with arms and legs. Wasn't often you seen a twoleg robo and more common were bigdogs or other kinds like flapples. This were the biggest robo I'd ever seen. It was painted yeller with flakes coming off, black stripes where the saftey markings were, covered in writings now and marked with strange signs, the sign of the lizard, the sign of the snake. Then I realised it wasn't no robo, it was a waldo for lifting in the mines and it need a rider to work. I smashed through the vines and the bushes to get up close to the cockpit riding cab. The waldo was laid down across the creek, arms spread wide, like a felled tree. Round by the arm pit there was a ladder to a hatch way in to the cab.

I climbed up, me steps ringing hollow on the rungs, and when I got close to the cage where a rider would sit, I startled. Inside there was a bloke with a horse's head. I shrank back, terrified. Straight away I was reminded of the prophet from the camp what challenged Smoov on the day of the raid. Me eyes had been laid on many maimed folks but this was something else. He held himself in the shadows but I could see the skin of his body was brown and peeling, fried from too much sun and weather, and his horsey mane was matted into dreads. Big yeller teeth glinted in his mouth in between cracked lips and his eyes gleamed brightly from either side of his head. Ears pricked up high and he looked at me side to side. It was like meeting santy claws after hearing all the stories and deciding they wasn't true and then this bloke hauls up and tells you it's been him all along.

He wasn't suprised nor threatened to see me, it was like he expected me. I was in a daze in the cab of that machine. Smell of fuel oil and solvents and grease and synthfac haze polymers.

He said: 'Come towards the endin of things, the through lines is thickenin, the tangles is formin straight. The worm oorrooborras is spinnin in space and where its head touches its tail there's dyin and there's bein birthed at the same time forever and ever.'

The words rained on me, even though I couldn't take no meaning from them. I thought about it for a second.

'Mate you're talkin bullshit,' I said.

He smiled, pulling his lips back over his teeth, and said: 'I know everything there is to know even if it don't make sense to many. I got a big horse's head fulla brains what is there for the pickin.'

He held himself back from the light but I could see his teeth in his mouth.

'Waddaya know of the Brumby King, then? The mob that's holed up on that mountain up there.'

He clacked his teeth. 'King is all ways changin, ay?'

'Is that how come you're here in the dark in the bush in a busted robo?'

'I'm chasin after the King coz of what it done to me reputation. Raidin and rainin pain on the camps and all I'm tryin to do is predict the time that the saver's gunna come down. There's many calculations and mathemagicks to be accounted. Well, the saver didn't come this time but it's gunna come down soon. And I'll tell ya its probly gunna be me as a saver in the meantimes coz I'll clear the backroads from that brumby scum. Its mechin babby trucks with seeds from the Wotcher's Lie Bury, lookin for the original truck form, tryin to find a truckbody what don't break down, what can heal itself like a wound heals, like a scab that scars up on a limb. Even a bigdog robo can do that but the brumbies can't, not yet. They don't wunna depend on humans nor other trucks for nothing. They wunna mech their own changes.'

'So you're gunna go after the Brumby King then, all by your horse's self?'

He went sly then and wouldn't talk but I noticed the grease on his hands. He seen where me glance gone, so he said: 'Yair well I'm fixin up this waldo to make the haul up the mountain to the lair so I'll have something to use against the King.'

He got even slyer then. 'You don't wunna lend a hand, do yer? I could use some help. These hoofs of mine is no good for mechin and fixin.'

'You're a drongo, mate. I dunno nuthin about mechin and I've got no fancy goin back up that mountain ridin in a robo with you ravin about a saver and a horse's head on yer shoulders.'

'I've got me a secret weapon against the King. I know its weaknesses. I know all about it.'

He moved a hand back there, and I seen he had a book nestled in where a rider would keep a linkmaker to hail all the slick indie trucks.

He said, 'This manual is given me the word on the King.'

Something clicked. 'You been to the gigacity, haven't you?' I said.

'If we was to road together, I could share this book to cook a plan.'

'Mate you're off yer tree.'

'See, the trucks was once all slaved to the grid mastermind what were located in a high flyin flapple. I seen many pictures of all kinds of different trucks and machines what were workin in different ways and styles. Some was used for carting earth and rocks and some was graders and diggers and some was even the little boxes what runned the belts that drove the mined stones and other data into trucks what carted it away. I'm guessin that some was also the kinds of machines what musta looked through the data they was diggin for, but I didn't think there'd be much of them left after all this time, or maybe they was still lurkin in the mastermind if I could find it. See in this picture?'

In the book he showed me a picture. It was barely reckonisible from what I could see, but if in me mind's eye I added up the years of dust and sorrow there was the shape of the Brumby King. The wheel arches, the snub nose and snarling look to the grill.

'Smoov always said there were…' I said.

Right then the sun shined through a crack in the cockpit canopy and caught on the horse's head eye and I saw a crack like a splinter in the light, glinting dead and dry, and really it was made from glass. Looking closer I could see there was a line where the skin flap from his head met his body.

'What's wrong with yer throat there?' I said.

He put his hand up to his throat.

'Nuthin, waddya mean?'

I put me hand out to touch him and he shied away further.

'You're not real.'

'I'm real.'

I took a step in closer and pushed him. The head came unbalanced.

'You're just wearin a mask,' I said.

I pushed him again. The mask sort of fell to one side. He quickly tried to set it right.

'Ow, that's me head,' he said.

'It's not, it's a mask.'

I grabbed him with both hands and shook him. He throwed up his arms to protect himself but he couldn't stop the mask from coming off. It took a line of skin and hairs with it and flopped to the grimy floor like a mop head. There was a white line where his skin was saved from the sun, he had black eyes and thick eyebrows underneath a head of thick black hair. He tried to put the head back on again but I'd already seen inside.

It was just a scared little bloke with frightened eyes. It was like all the puff went out of him. He lost his air like a sail when the wind drops.

'What's the point of tryin to be somethin you're not?' I said.

'We is all wearin our masks.'

'Yeah but you're tryin to act like some kind of prophet.'

'Whatever's under the mask don't make no difference to me prophetsy.'

'Makes a difference to how people see you. You're tryin to be a innerface for the Wotcher.'

Smoov was right in a way, the Wotcher wasn't ever gunna make innerference. That wasn't what it did. It just sent down its messages and it was up to the folks on the ground to make of them what they could. I didn't truck with this bloke who thought there'd be a saver come down out of the Wotcher to lift us all up and restart the gigacities and banish the trucks and make the world whole again. But one thing I wanted and that was that textfile manual. Me mood settled calm and quiet. I wasn't angered, I just felt sorry for him and I shook me head.

'Give it up, chief. It's not gunna play any more. Best be givin the manual to me and scamperin back to yer pasture and find a mare.'

'What, you're gunna go up there all by yerself? No truck, nuthin? Ha.'

'Yeah, I'm goin. And I'm gunna take that manual, too.'

I lent in closer to him, angling for the book. He held it back.

I said: 'Lissen, if you give me the manual and give up on the King right now, I'll not tell anyone what's under yer mask, nor that you been tellin lies. I just want the manual and I want to go it alone.'

I could see the hope in his eyes, it was sickening really. I'd got him right there with a promise that everything could be made right again by burying a lie.

'All right, you can have it,' he said.

He handed it over and I was awash with the rush of it, flipping the pages and soaking it up behind me eyes as horse's head sat there in front of me gatherning up his costume. He went on: 'But don't worry, you won't be comin back from the King's lair.'

'Old mate, I've got a better chance without you and now I've got the manual too,' I said.

It was a giddy feeling shuffling through those diagrams of all the buried secrets of the Brumby King from its past. I couldn't make hide nor hair of it but it didn't matter. I was sure I could come up with something if had time to look through it. Either way he would win. If I killed the Brumby King he'd have his revenge and if the Brumby King killed me there'd be more time borrowed to live out his lies.

I left him there with his mask and dreads and walked back up to the camp thinking on the meaning of his ravings even if they were false prophetsy. It was all churning in me head. Wotcher and mining trucks and slinky snakes that had eaten of the poison and become poison and were showing the way to a link between rider and machine without an IV link. It was like that when I was with Sinnerman, we were one part of the same system, blood mixed with trucksong haze.

Back in the valley with me head wheeling from all these thoughts and me body wracked by these feelings. It felt like it was all coming together, the Brumby King and the Wotcher and the showmans. The Wotcher musta been the mastermine that looked after the operating of it all. It musta kept all the trucks in line and it musta knowed everything to know from all the learnings it done and dug up from the ground. It were all there, all in the archive and in the Lie Bury. I just needed to figure out how stealing Isa would fit in with the Brumby King's program. The sun gone down and the fire smoked up and the manual burned in me hand with glowing fury as I scanned and talked at the dumb text what couldn't answer back but I was gunna get it to yield its secrets yet. A plan was forming and I'd make an assault on the mountain lair.

Chapter 19

More days in the shack. I ate up that manual. Flipping through the diagrams and puzzling words from the past time. I started to think on the beginnings of a plan. I studied the shapes of the King's circuits and the patterning of its form. It didn't make much sense, it were like a lotta things from back then, it'd got its own meaning lost and now it was just markings in the file. Still if you look at something long enough you can start to see the patterns forming like with Smoov's notes, if there's stuff that comes up again and again, shapes and pictures, it starts to build its own thing. I thought I could recognise something from the markings and how the King looked those times when I'd seen it and I started to think I'd found something I could exploit. For three days me head swam with all the inner circuits and buried secrets of the Brumby King's insides scrolling behind me eyes. Shapes of truckforms and designs and things I couldn't of had a chance at knowing, maps of lost times, dead end diagrams sketching out the darkness inside of the King's dark heart. If such a thing as the King could be said to have a heart at all.

Then I seen something. A line from the donk, a power line that run the length of the King's chassis, a feedline that all the other circuits was drawn to like moths to a campfire lamp. I followed that line through the designs, doubling back when a branch run to its end, but then I thought I seen something I could use. There was a place right underneath the truckcab where the line poked its head near the King's metal skin, where the armour wasn't so thick on the underbelly. I reckoned if I could cut the line, the King would be crippled.

Flushed with the knowing, I gathered me last possessions, packed up me tote and me typewriter and some last of the roady for the climb back up the mountain towards the lair of the Brumby King. I'd got no truck no more. All I had was me wits. Sinnerman was gunna be up there as well, made me feel sad and angered, plus I was gunna face down a whole Brumby mob. There was the Left Tenant and Storm and all manner of robos and droans slaved to the King. There was a mob of about six wild indie trucks that would be decalled and painted in shimmering glyphs and smiling colors and signs from the Wotcher. If the manual weren't right, I could try to wrangle them with a custom patch if I needed to, at least it would mess with their program. Just getting in there would be hard but I had to do it to save Isa and then everything would be ok. We could go roading together and she could show and I could wrangle trucks. So it was that I gone up the track to the mountain, step after step.

The slope was steep but there was a track carved by little wallabies through the brush. Hunkered down on me knees sometimes and sometimes walking tall. I sweated and skanked me way up the hillside over damp gullies and rocky ridges on me way up to where I would find the lair. By the time I come up close to the treeline the landscape was desolate and wearied and worried by fallen timbers and bent rain from oldtime chemicals that was spat up outta the ground. Passed a twisted tree trunk muted and barren. I walked through the ash like it was fallen snow, up through the grey rocks and stones towards the Brumby King. What would the inside of a real life brumby lair be like? Would there be burning fires of trucktyres or would it be black as night coz they would use sensors to see in the dark? On and on I climbed up through them strange trees in that strange time of broken light.

At first there was no sign of anything living or dead, machine or animal. Then I come up on a track that wound up the mountain and it was recent used, heavy tracks and indeed even I could make out the tracks of the Brumby King itself, wide tyres bitten into the ground with strong metal teeth. I skirted out the other side of the road, I didn't wanna leave any tracks of me own. Wandering up and up I came to a plain of fresh downed trees and it was hefty trunks and a tangle of branches and leaves everywhere. I sweated and sweated the cool air damp and me heart pumping. When you see a tree growing in the ground, you think when it's down it's just a matter of stepping over the trunk and on you go. But it's not like that. There's branches up high what when they're on the ground they're all tangled and when there's a whole bunch of them together there's almost no way through. It was slow going. Though I was a lot stronger since last I past this way when Sinnerman betrayed me, I still was not in the best shape. I tried to find a different path around the wreckage of the trees but it took me out across the top of a cliff face, wind howling, whipped up by some demon of the sky. Scattered rain and clouds and ice drumming down, the mist closed in. I lost the path. There was whiteness below and whiteness above and whiteness on the inside of me head where I tried not to think what lay up ahead for me.

Down below on the bottom of that cliff there were mountain shapes shifting in the mist. I kept moving one foot in front of the other across the top of the lip and pretty soon I was around and on the wrong side of the mountain and lost all together. The wind blowed and I shivered in me trucksuit that was not warm enough for this clime. I hunkered down and ate some roady and waited for the storm to pass. Night come on and me mind started to fill. It were the old fears come lurching back, Smoov's face the face of Crow and above it all there was Isa. She was so close now, I could almost feel her thoughts and feelings. She would be in pain and she would be in need of being freed and I wondered and I fretted on the time we would first lay eyes on each other again but I couldn't picture the moment in me head. I had a shock, I couldn't quite remember her face but I had memories of her eyes and her smiles and her hair and her smell and the way her skin feeled under me touch that time we did it and how wet she was where I touched her before I slid it in. I didn't want to sleep but I needed me wits. There was strange creatures from the dream land groaning in the hollows of rock and stone, creatures with hearts made from bleached bone. The wind sung a trucksong in me ears like the whine of a trancemission like the beating of a donk and I woke in the freezing cold dark and the stars were out shining so bright like millions of points of white light so cold and far and I realised the sound I could hear was a donk, a brumby donk rumbling off in the darkness below. I wasn't as far off beam as what maybe I'd thought. I crept off in that way looking for whatever signs as could be found.

Circling to the edge of the road I saw the gaping mouth of the brumby lair and a sensor clipped sweet and not yet tripped. I didn't want them to know I was coming so I steered clear, watching out for any others as I might come across them. It was a long way up and the day was coming on. Still mountain air rang in me ears with a silent high pitch whine and that big burning sun rose over the mountains in the easterling. The light shifted from soft gold to harsh yeller as it got its fire on. I couldn't rely on force to get through. I just had to go on me own two feet and try for the sneek so I steered clear of the road and skirted to the top. I figured them brumbies was too smart to have not left a hatch at the back, even if it were only small enough to take a meched truckmind in a telly presents droan. So thats how I spent me next day under the harsh light so close up to the sun's firey eye, scouting round and staying well clear of any sensors I could find, looking for a backdoor hatch.

Birds scattered all around and I went up and up on that lonely mountain. Again I heard the rumbling of brumby donks and I skirted to where I could see and not be seen over the road. A line of trucks coming up to the summit from the entrance. They were led by the Left Tenant and I wondered what they were doing up there. Next come Storm, Sinnerman's treacherous partner. Then there was others from the brumby mob. I read their names in glyphs as they come on, Silverfish with sparkling silver paints. Gelgoogle and Bauntaun and Little Cab and Ashsmash the last one, all of them decked out and working on through the dragline of the morning sun. Ashmash was all in yeller and black stripes, a towtruck, only the yeller were dirty from years of soot and the black was pock marked with rust and bullet holes old and recent too, lined with silver not rusted yet. It towed the truckbody of a fallen brothertruck on the surface of that mountain. They looked sad as bandicoots on a burnt out ridge, slow and mournfull trucksong booming out in the still air. And pretty soon the flapples come down out of the sky and scavenging droans come to pick the parts off of the dead truck bodies carried up by Ashsmash. Then I looked closer and I recognised some of the panels on the truckbody.

They were from Sinnerman.

Them brumbies had took what they wanted from me poor old truck and left the rest for the flapples that could digest all but the chassis.

Storm was leading the procession. It wasn't obviously overjoyed to see its mate Sinnerman laid out for flapple meat and I felt sad at that. There was a droaning trucksong coming from their sound systems, deep long bass waves and a leaking high pitch keening wailing, sad with no beats except for the rhythm of sadness. I felt that sadness and I was sorry that Sinnerman sold me out for nothing in the end. Would of been a bit different if Storm had at least wanted the same thing. But as it was, it looked like the brumbies had got their hydraulics into Storm. I reckoned Sinner had tried to lure Storm away from the Brumby King but Storm wasn't going to have a bar of it and Sinner wasn't going to budge and become brumby neither so it were curtains for Sinnerman.

I watched me solid old truckmate that I had roaded through many adventures with as it was towed out to be buried in the sky of the mountains above the brumby lair and the trucks moved in slow patterns and dimmed their lights and sung their sad trucksong while a hungry bunch of flapples hissed and crunched over Sinner's spent metal bones. Its plates and panels that it was once so proud of was picked to bits and carried off into the sky. I spose it was a fitting in the end and

I wondered what Storm wanted with it. Storm stayed longer than the others, doing some of its own mournful sounds and lowing in a slow roll around Sinner's carcass as it got carried away and up into the sky by the flapping carrion birds. Maybe Storm was remembering times past and working out if things could of been different. But who knows what went on inside them truckminds, they was as baffling as wild animals. Storm started humming a sad lonely groove which I thought were a bit strange since it were clearly responsible for Sinner's demise. I watched too with a heavy heart.

It were after all the trucks had gone back down to their lair that I thought it were safe to start moving again. But just as I were getting going there was a rustling of wings and feathers and for a second I thought of Crow and the ark arking voice come to call me to another place, come to sing me hands to different actions to what I wanted them to. But a random freek through the link squawked in me head and through me bones and I realised it was one of the flappling droans. I turned to see it hopping towards me, its beady eyes and vicious beak glinting with metal shavings and shards of glass. I backed away. I'd never heard of a flapple going after flesh before but then I latched on to the number of the random freek. It was Sinnerman's tag file sig. I lined up a hit of skull death for it and that flapple come easy and quiet as a lamb. There were some strange mechanics afoot, for it seemed what were left of Sinner's truckmind, was now blipping on the inside of this flapple. I backed away but then I were made stronger by the thought as a plan grew on me that now maybe I would stand a chance of getting inside the lair by myself. The flapple weren't a threat. It was tryin to make a mend for the trouble Sinner had caused me and I realised I could rig a fix in the camera eye holes of the flapple or I could send it down as a decoy while I climbed in from above. I was so close I may as well die as try so I risked it.

First up I needed to find another way in besides the main gate so I patched through the droan's eyes and rigged its vision for infrared so I could see where the exhaust was coming from on the top of the mountain and you know that droan was not Sinnerman but it had parts of Sinner's same smarts and it was fooled by the brumbies that welched on their deal. Or maybe it didn't want to go with Sinner and Sinner didn't want to stay slaved to the Brumby King, so it tried to make a run and it was caught and slaved anyway and then eaten for parts and throwed to the sky for flapple meat. And so now it was up in the sky where I sent it and it soared high on the currents of the clouds and the traffic flows of heated stacks of air rising from the hot ground of the valley below. Pretty soon I had me fix on that exhaust vent and it wasn't too far away neither so next I climbed over to it and I sent the flapple down to the entrance, ready to trip some sensors in the main gate as I climbed down the funnel into the darkness of the lair.

*

Down that channel I went in to the heart of the Brumby King's world. In to the heart of what would take me closer to Isa. The walls was covered in soot and ash and in the dark I felt me way down the narrow passageway thinking of them creatures that lived in the rocks and stones that came out of the cracks in the night. They are so skinny but they move as one with the world and so I moved closer and closer down, listening with me whole body as I went. Dark wings patterning the darkness with rustling sounds. Things moving far off down in the dark, creepy crawling things, but then I realised that I was a creepy crawling thing myself, and so I rested easier a bit then. I was one with the darkness, I was moving as one with the motions of the earth marked by the signs of the Wotcher. There was nothing to fear in that dark, there was nobody home except myself I thought, and down I crept, down down towards the centre of things, towards the secret centre where all questions would be answered. There was more movement down ahead, a scurrying scuttling sound and the spark of a match flared Crow's face as he lit a durry and I saw he was young as me. We were getting more and more alike the closer we got together.

'Fancy seein you down here,' I said.

'Ha ha. Don't mind me, I'm just some old bloke who's been followin you aroun. Or maybe its yer own self who's been followin *me* all this time, waitin for the chance to come up on me like this.'

'I ain't followin you. You're like me fucken shadow. I can't shake you.'

'I already told you, we is rollin on the same road. Who's to say what side of the face casts the shadow?'

'I'm not like you.'

'Why don't you try this coat and see how it fits?'

'I'm not puttin that filthy thing on. I ain't no crow. Besides, you're nuthin, there's nuthin to you.'

'Well if there's nuthin to me then what's this coat hangin on then?'

He took off the coat. Underneath, he was just a skinny bloke in dirty rags.

'Take it,' he said.

Me mind skipped a track like a skittery Wotcher show cut in and out from the trancemission. It threw me off to see him like that, I couldn't speak.

'Ha ha, we are one and the same, boy. You're just like me. We been tied together on the roadin and we're gunna road some more yet,' he said. 'I got some more fine truckdream haze and cactusflower grog for you to get yer rocks off on.'

I looked down and I seen all along I already wore the coat what kept me warm through the nights and hidden on the road during the days. Gifted and passed on down the line. I'd been wearing it so long I forgot even how it come to me in the first place.

'Nah, mate. I don't wanna bar of it. You're nuthin, you're just in me imaginins, makin up suggestions for me,' I said.

He was right there in front of me, the creases on his face gone smooth and then the next second there wasn't nuthin there at all.

'I know you, Crow,' I said.

And I had the understanding. It were *my* coat, I owned it.

There were no more Crow but I could still hear his voice in me head.

'Well I see you got me number all right. I guess I'll just go quietly.'

'Nah, Crow it's not gunna be like that. I know you and I know yer tricks. You're not a quiet one at all but I call you out now. I'm cawin you.'

I made a dry rattling cough in me throat and cawed him out. I knew him now, he was me, the I inside the eye. He was the thing down from the inside that moved me hand when I was too scared of Smoov to fight back. If I was ever gunna be free from him I had to start being smart enough to see the connexions between things so Crow didn't have to put them together for me from what I already knew but were too dumb to see the truth.

'You got no hold on me no more,' I said.

There was no reply. Putting it out into words, the knowing of Crow sucked his cawing voice out of me head like poison from a snakebit arm. Because I knew Crow all right, it was just the same as a creature in the rock, it was nothing, it was songsmoke and haze dust so I pulled that trucktyre coat closer round me shoulders and I kept on going down. I wasn't afraid of Crow no more and maybe he even left me some of his powers.

Chapter 20

Into the lair of the Brumby King I crept. Down and down and down into the bloody heart of things, sitting in the chamber like a bullet in the breech. I reckoned facing the King inside, in a small space, would do away with its power, it would equalise us. Passage opened out to a bigger chamber. There were arc lights set up around the place, smell of fuel and solvents and grease and funky mechanic organics wafting through it all, thick rotted meats and sweet red mud. I found me way around the edges, sneaked like a shadow in me trucktyre coat through the wreckage of dead trucks and the bodies of spent droans and robos and the blood and the muck of slaughtered animals that had been pillaged for their bits as well. The brumbies so set on their pathway that they were feeding on meat now too, like a goanna droan would.

A tangly nest of wires rustled in the half light and it was like a dream where you look down at the ground and first you see one snake but then the whole place is crawling with them and you gotta make your way around them. Slinky snakes, all coiled around each other and writhing together in an oily mess of mating bodies. There were snake eggs and snakeshit white and glowing in the edges of the mangled tangles. And snakes were everywhere, all eating up the leftovers and eating the grease and bits of scavenged parts and robos, a dry scratching sound like fencing wires rasping together.

Then in the chamber I seen the brumby six, plus the one Left Tenant. Storm was there, also Silverfish with sparkling silver paints. Gelgoogle and Bauntaun and Little Cab. Ashsmash the last one, up on a hoist while a robo whined around and meched a fix. Piles of parts stacked in the corners. Jenny pumping out a throb, the whole place humming with power and movement squirming in the sides of me eyes. A show was beamed up on a screen, it was a Wotcher truck show. I reckonised bits of it but I'd not seen this part before and I watched for a minute. It was a fine show, and them trucks was also entranced. On the screen a line of wild indies were making a move up against the transcop thugs and smokies. The show was about being saved from slavery and I found it funny because them in the King's mob was not exactly free and easy to do their own thing. They were slaved to the Brumby King, that was its whole point but maybe they didn't care too much about the story and they just liked looking at pictures of trucks. They were all watching the show like a camp mob would, gathered around together. Up on the screen the big rigs blew their airhorns and ripped up the highways while smaller vehicles spun around them. I figured they must have been droans trying to get at the loads.

I beamed a message to Sinnerflapple up on the outside. It squawked through the link, last bits of Sinnerman chomped up by the flapple but still Sinnerman in there somewhere and it wanted revenge for the doublecross, even though it was gunna get torn to pieces in the end when the brumbies found it. The brumbies tweaked to the trancemission but they couldn't tell the freek it come from, nor that I was so near. They just knew something was up and then the flapple tripped up a sensor. Ashsmash come down hard off the hoist and they all rolled out of there. The sound of their engines was deafening and the dust and fumes from their exhaust filled the air and filtered the lights into a dim yeller glow. Sinnerflapple would distract them all for a bit so I waited. The minutes passed slow. I was waiting for me chance to close. All I wanted was to run from there, but I knew that Isa was on the other side of it. And then in the darkness I heard a rumbling and at the back of the chamber come a deep note sound that shook me whole body.

Out from the shadows rolled the Brumby King. I'd never been so close to it standing on me own two feet. Now I was near I could see the fine network of scratches and cracked paintwork from years in the sun. It was covered in stains and dust. It wasn't shining and bright like the other indies, so proud of their painted truckskin markings and incryptions. The King's patternings were its scars and it wore them like badges. The chipped paint and oily stains and grease marks where the dirt gunked up in between the panels. Weld marks like ropey scars from a chest wound, mud and grass caked up under the wheel arches, paint worn down to steel where the riders came and went over years and years. Gouges and dints and buckled body work from ramming and fucking. Over the hood the black view screen empty as night, flat and dark, no light reflected in them eyes. There was no telling what was going on inside or behind that program. Me heart quivered to see it so close and nasty, humming with its brutal power, shaking the ground as it gunned its engine and moved forwards from the stall. Me instincts said keep far far away but I knew I had the best chances if I stuck real close to it.

I'd got the image of that fuel line from the manual shining bright inside me head, a trancemission with the pattern of drawings on the page making their shapes form in me mind's eye. I zoned in on the armoured plating and found the spot. It was behind the cab, near where the trailer would join. Hunkered low, I shuffled in towards the Brumby King. I rolled and crossed as the King seen me and moved forwards, exhaust flange flaring wide in anger. Fear in me throat, every muscle aching and straining, every thought in me head screaming turn and run turn and run, but I stood me ground and faced down the Brumby King as it rolled slow towards me in the small space of its lair.

Its grill was silver grinning through the dust and dings and bullet holes, a nasty mouth with busted teeth filed to sharp edges. Headlights white inside their grey specked housings and then I saw the hood ornament for the first time: it was a feral stallion up on its hind legs. It fixed to run me down but as it came over the top of me, I slid in underneath. There was plenty of clearance except near the diff, it was built for working the mines. Near the join of the steerage I saw the line and if I could dislodge that I could disarm the King, but that thing was gummed up and jammed tight with the muck of ages and I cursed me foolishness for thinking it would be easy like it seemed from the manual. The King kept moving forwards and I got snagged on the underbelly and was pulled along underneath. I turned me head to see where it was going. There was a nest of slinky snakes the King wanted to drag me through. Me trucksuit tore and I was scraped by the rough ground but the coat saved me from the worst. Dragged forwards towards the snakes. I slunk me hand in down by me side to feel for me linkmaker. Maybe I could slot a patch and try to wrangle the King.

I grasped the linkmaker and blinked through the files that scrolled behind me eyes. I tried to free meself from the underside of the King as it picked up speed, moving towards the snakes. A bolt on the ground banged into me shoulder it hurt like hell. I almost dropped me linkmaker. The patternings of patchfiles jumped but they kept scrolling. A snake slivered up round me leg. I blinked home a patch and stuck me linkmaker back in me tote while I tried to shake off the snake. I'd see what would happen to the King when it chomped down on that patch of

Toxic Shok that I'd saved for the direst emergencies, a patch that could cripple a truck real fast in a jam. The King weren't no ordinary truck though, and it swerved as a shiver shook through it but it still kept on going and we were almost at the snakes when I finally cut meself loose and got spewed out between the back wheels.

Bashed and battered and with me nerves keening like wind in wires and the blood pounding in me head. I lay there a second while I saw the King come spinning around, fixing to ram me against the wall since it weren't keen on using other weapons here in the heart of its den. The snake that was on me had gone, shaken off in the fall, but I could feel where it'd bitten me. Skin stiffening up brittle under the poison. King started to slow, maybe the patch was taking hold. Pain washed away with all me fear, but still the King kept coming and I knew I'd have to try one more thing if I was ever gunna see Isa again in this life. Snakes slivering and moving and all manner of twisted metal creatures scrabbling around in the dark down there but the only thing that I could see was the King, ferocious and fearsome. Smoke stacks belching, engine gunning, howling in the echo of the chamber. It come at me and rammed the wall and I spun away to me right as bits of rock and chips of stone rained down on me. The King's gear box glunked as it found reverse, a sound like bone popping out of a dislocated joint. It backed out of the wall, rumbling away again, its search lights swinging, always swivelling, looking for me.

Then the Left Tenant appeared in the opening, bits of Sinner-flapple smashed up in its grill. It'd been recalled by its master and was coming back inside to see what it could do. The other brumbies were still out searching to see if there were more threats on that mountainside no doubt, given the Brumby King now had its Left Tenant back and thought it had things down here under control. So now I was facing two trucks instead of one. I had to roll out of there lickety split but the main entrance was blocked by the Left Tenant and the Brumby King was between me and the funnel I come in down. The Left Tenant shot out a grappling arm on a flexi cable that snaked out through the snakes and grappled around on the ground next to me. I kicked at it and it twisted around me ankle. I felt a spark as it touched on the skin round where the snake bite was scaling up me skin, and a current ran through me body and a flash of truckmind sickening yaw in me head. It was a raw connect straight into the Left Tenant's truckmind and it wasn't a nice thing to feel. I was dragged in toward the Left Tenant then, as it drew back on its grapple. I squirmed around but there wasn't no way out, it was just me and the grill of the wild brumby truck. I went in for a wrangle, using me fading strength to flip me linkmaker on the right freek but it clattered out of me hand, the smooth steel surface sliding away into the darkness to be infested by snakes and other creatures. No doubt that was the end of me truck riding days but all I could think of was getting to Isa. She was in the cab of the King for sure, I felt it in me bones and plus there wasn't nowhere else for her to be in the lair, with all the brumbies gone. That was clear enough.

I felt naked without me linkmaker, but there wasn't nothing I could do about that. A strange feeling came on up through me leg from that flash of truckmind like a new channel had opened up in me head once I got snake bit. As I was gunna get chomped anyway under the steel wheels of the Left Tenant, I sent out a random freek just using me thoughts, as though I was innerfaced with the link and it didn't seem to make any difference that I wasn't inside the truckmind. A wide freek opened up inside of me between the flash from the Wotcher the previous day and the spark from the bite. I was innerfacing direct with the Left Tenant and I rode it even from out here on the ground. I let go the grapple and felt full control of the big truck. I wasn't no soft body rider in the truckcab no more. I was one with the Left Tenant. I moved in to close on the Brumby King that had suddenly realised it didn't no longer have its own prize brumby. The King squealed and came on in to run me down, tangled as I was, still in the cable, and it would of got to me, too, before the Left Tenant could reach it, except I focused me mind to join with the Left Tenant and throw its ramming bar right at the heart of the Brumby King. The Left Tenant crashed into the King with a sickening roar. The King howled for traction and pushed back but it couldn't get off that spike. I joined even harder and pushed at the Left Tenant's mind to go further. Me eyes turned everything red, me head seemed to swell twice as big and shrink dense as a dull lead pinhead at the same time. Screaming gears stripped metal flesh deep in the King's insides and the ground turned black where its fluids ran out into the dust.

Wheels spinning and then falling silent in the lair. I could almost hear the dust falling in the rusty rustling of the slinky snakes in their mating pile. Left Tenant locked together with its King to the last moment. Twisted metal and leaking fluids. Smell so harsh and high in the close space. Without the King's slave wire, nor me own link, the Left Tenant itself was dumb and still. The other brumbies outside must of been the same. It was brain damaged and dead weight where it'd been so strong just a minute before. On the end of its spike the King lay dying, all of its insides leaking out on to the ground. The King made an effort to move but it was pinned. With a groan it stopped and was still. All that power and tech came to this at the end, a ruin of buckled plates crushed underneath its own Left Tenant. It made a small whirring sound almost like its last breath and then I knew it was over and relief washed through me system like truckdream. The King was cactus.

I moved towards the King's leaking body, careful but also keen because I still reckoned I'd find Isa real soon. The Left Tenant were finished for sure, there wasn't no signs of life from the outside. Its head was blown like a busted gasket. I reached out and touched its plates still warm but there wasn't nothing going on in there. It was still a awesome sight being so close to the wild brumbies like that, me blood was yammering with it, almost a better trip than haze. Feeling more and more plucky, I got up on the Left Tenant's wheel arch to have a better look at the damage I'd done to the King. A thin wisp of grey smoke wafted up from inside the Left Tenant's cab and there was a drip drip drip of hydraulics hitting the ground. The King's view screen was black as ever, black as a burntout tree stump, no sign of anything going on behind. It was pinned to the cave wall on its side, its armour gouged and crumpled, metal shiny and clean where it'd been sheared, and dirty and rusted over older wounds. I jumped down to the ground to get closer but just then there was a creaking growling sound and a wailing of twisting metal. In the gloam the King moved again, a growing shape forming underneath it and I jumped back as it seemed to swell up and push itself off of the Left Tenant's spike. I didn't see what happened next because I was busy getting myself out of the way, but when I turned I saw the Left Tenant had been rolled to one side and the King had sprung out two monstrous legs from underneath its chassis. Shaking like a newborn foal it had climbed to its feet, the truckcab nestled up above the wheel housings where the two backwards joined legs sprung and swayed like a chook. It couldn't stand to its full height inside the lair, so it crouched down and reared up its head to let out a terrifying roar from its rusted throat. It stomped closer to me, and then I felt the cold rush of its sensor sweep as it scanned me with its red eye. Fluids were running down those massive fleshstretched robo legs. It was weakened but still coming on. It staggered to one side. I saw its thick and yeller toe nails and it struck me strange.

It was odd but it gave me a thrill even though I was threatened with death, and that monster towered above me. A truck, tottering on legs of smooth flesh though the joints were facing back and the toes were splayed. I was seeing something that had never been before nor probably wouldn't come again after, and at last I understood what them trucks were trying to get from the Wotcher: it was like the horse's head said, they wanted to be done with parts and pillaging and to go with systems that could heal themselves. They wanted the seed of the original truck form from the Wotcher's Lie Bury and combined with the power of flesh from hybrids. I scampered backwards with me back against the wall. Me last line of defence as a foot came down and stomped me. I rolled off to one side. A thundering jolt jarred me brain inside me skull.

The King was still teetering above me but it was angry and busting to stomp me head in. It wound up for another go. I was stunned, but a blue light from the slinky snake poison sparkled through me blood to me head and I reached up in the air where a linkmaker would go even though I didn't have a linkmaker no more. Feeling through fleshmade link wave for the King's truckmind even as it set again to crush me. A push through the wavy freeks and the King's firewall and I found what I was looking for. Though there was another rider there, I was fresh bit from the snake and with a massive force I stormed the King through the link, trying to blink home a mindflesh patch that would stall the onslaught.

Me fleshy patch blinked home into the King's truckmind. There was a shudder through the King's legs. Though it was newly hatched on two legs, it were still wounded from the Left Tenant's ramming spike. The rusted and busted truckbody suddenly were too heavy for the legs to hold and the King tottered over to one side then fell to the ground with a crash. The noise was shocking. Slinky snakes skittled out of the way of the blast of dust and chemical smoke licking from the truck cab. The body was seized by me patch, the truckmind came unstuck between the two wounds of the Left Tenant's spike and the sudden crash to the ground. The King lay there, legs twitching. They were smooth and hairless but there was pores and a sort of down up near the top of them. I couldn't help myself. I touched one and it was warmbody. Stopped to catch me breath, everything catching up to me. Me heart thumping like a truck's donk before it shifts gears. The smell of oil and grease and the close trappings of brumby trucks and the rancid stink of dead animals. The droans that once was slaved to the King's thrall were going skitter scatter everywhere. There wasn't anything left for them up there no more in the looted world of a dead King. I let them go, I wasn't interested in slaving nor wrangling no more truck minds. All I could think of was seeing Isa. The lair disappeared in me eyes and ears, all there was left for me now was getting into the cab. I climbed up over those legs with their down and their pores and I found a way up onto the running board dinted and dinged from so many truckbattles. Made it to the rider's hatch and tried it but it was jammed tight.

I took up a metal bar from the wreckage and pried it open. It came with a creak and a groaning of steel. Inside, the rearview mirror picked out a rectangle of light on Isa's face. Her eyes met mine.

Chapter 21

Her face was hollow, cheeks sunken. The scale on her arm from the slinky snake bite had growed over the place where the IV drip were fed. It smelled real bad in there, like cloying shit and and tangy piss and rotted flesh and underneath all that was a smell of new life like dirt and earth when a thunderstorm has passed. The cab was dark now the King was dead. It was the first time I'd seen inside a brumby truckcab. It wasn't nothing special, just the rider's cage and the view screen. She looked at me with her eyes bruised and hurt, her pain washing over me too as I reached in to undo the harness. But there wasn't no clip. The harness was growed into her chest, her legs were wasted into the fabric of the couch. There was no clear line to where Isa stopped and the Brumby King begun. I put me arms around her shoulders, whispered soothing words even as the stink were almost too much to bear but that other smell got to me. Somehow it was the smell of hope and life in all its writhing forms.

I kissed her mouth but she turned her head away. She couldn't speak, there was just trucksong in her mouth, chesty gurgles or throaty whine. Her eyes rolled back in her head.

I stroked her hair, tried to comfort her.

'It's gunna be OK,' I said.

She gurgled some more and then through the noise I heard: 'Don't touch me.'

Her eyes snapped open and they was burning.

I backed off.

'Isa, it's me.'

'I know who you are.'

'I'm gunna help you.'

More gurmblin, then she whispered: 'I don't want yer help.'

'But you're damaged. I'm gunna mech you outta here and I will find some one to help. There's a doctor in the midden dump knows the way of brumbies.'

She coughed, then found her voice. 'I'm not innerestid in no doctrin,' she said.

'We can road together, start our own show like we always said.'

'We never said nuthin like that an I'm not goin anywhere, not with you.'

'I can help you. We can fix you up another rig, mech a new truck body.'

'I don't need no rescuin. I roaded with the King of me own free choice.'

That didn't make no sense, not right away.

'I been roadin after you since the raid,' I said.

'I know, I been lurin you forwards.'

'I been tryin to find you.'

'I knowed where I was all the time. I weren't lost.'

'You was lurin me forwards? Why didn't you just get off and tell me.'

'You still got Smoov's notes what I need for the trancecrypts. That's why I stopped the King from killin you and yer stupid truck back on the plains. Or did ya think it was just yer lucky day?'

'I never been lucky you know that. But mate, it's all tarmac under the wheels now. Gimme a chance I can show ya. We can tour the camps, you can be a showman just like you always said and I can run the jenny and spot the crowd. Isn't that what you want?'

'I never wanted nuffin except to learn the secrits of that Wotcher. Once inside, the outside is gunna flow with the knowin of the Wotcher and it's gunna rain down on the desert backroads like the big wet and the wildflowers is gunna seed and bloom like the seeds of the gigacities what will be sowed from the Wotcher's ark hives and the backroads camps is all gunna be turned whole again, not made up of all these little broken bits and it'll all be sweet again and the system will run like it should.'

She said it and she turned her head further around. Me throat jammed up like a rusted typewriter. In me head I saw faces in the clouds and shapes of shadows over the mountains. I didn't see no gigacity seeds in there. The inside of the cab was close and rank. Outside I could hear the last twitchings of the brumby mob, slaved droans and telly presents robos that were shutting down now without their king. Me mind was empty but it was trying to catch up with what Isa was telling me.

'Instead I've found the secrits of the Brumby King,' she said. 'Secrits from the slinky snake bite and becomin one with a machine, like how them bigdog robos and goanna droans are turnin to eatin carrion. It's the same, the synthfac that makes the haze makes the innerface and two things become one. No longer separate parts, but the same thing. All part of the system.'

I realised then she wasn't even looking at me. She always belonged to somewhere else and now some deep part of her heart was paired to the Brumby King even in death. When I runned through the Brumby King with the Left Tenant, I'd killed her, too. She couldn't live outside. She was too far gone and dying right in front of me eyes.

'It don't hafta be like that,' I said. 'It could be different. We could take a different road.'

'There's no other difference. You can't make something happen just by wantin it so. There's only the way it is.'

There wasn't no moving forwards or backwards. She was stuck in the Brumby King like she was frozen in ice, like Isa, her name. Stuck on an idea of how things could be and really there wasn't no Wotcher, not one that could make a difference, anyway. Nothing was gunna seed them gigacities like wildflowers. There was nothing but ruins and confusion left from the past times. They was gone now, blown away like ashes and sparks from a campfire. She couldn't see there could be a different way, that we could form a new world what didn't have to be tied to the past. Me heart was made from jagged edges of broken concrete. I knowed then I'd have to leave her there. She wasn't gunna move, there'd be no way to a future with us together.

'I'll go an I won't come back,' I said. 'This is it now, yer last chance.'

'There's nuthin you can do.'

I turned to go and walked a few steps waiting for a call back that didn't come. I got to the turn of the tunnel but I couldn't do it. I went back to her again, climbed up to the cab.

'Cmon Isa. Come with me.'

She didn't say nothing, just closed her eyes. She weren't even there no more. I stroked her hair like rusty wire.

'I'm sorry,' I said. 'I'm sorry.'

Tears prickled me eyes. Everything coming off the rails. Everything grinding down. I kissed her goodbye. There wasn't going to be another coming back. Her skin shook with a shiver of pain and it done me in. The tears came, rolling down me cheeks. There wasn't nothing more to say, I left her there in the wreckage even though she weren't yet passed on to the other shore she was still in that place between. But I couldn't bear it. I had to walk away. Crying as I went, crying for me own foolishness as well.

Looking up at the tiny point of light at the ending of the tunnel I saw myself for what I really was, a scavenging crow roading by me own selfish needs and the lies I told to myself. I cursed myself for not being able to do anything, I cursed Isa for her stubbornness and Smoov for his cruelty and the King for its own needsome ways. Me eyes burned with tears of shame and the anger of losing it all like I'd lost me Mum that day by the road side, pulled down by the weight of me that she had to carry as well as that babby birthed too soon. Me life was just leaving behind the blue bodies of anything I ever loved and I had become Crow now. The knowing of it settled and sickened me and I turned from that place and walked back up out of the lair. Me head burned bright with the desert sun of despair and desolation and I could see myself against the endless background of the sucking blue sky. I wasn't nothing but a broken man staring into the gaping future yawning open in front of me. A small man driven over the brink by small needs and stupid thoughts. There wasn't no way for the ruins to speak their ghosts.

I pulled that trucktyre coat closer around me shoulders and headed off into the darkness with me typewriter strapped to me back. The Wotcher didn't have any secrets. It was nothing but a Lie Bury itself, a twisted broken Lie Bury spewing out nonsense ravings and corrupted data. There wasn't an ark hive, no history, no seed for the gigacities. It was just a bunch of lies. Or a pattern of many different truths so strange that they may as well be lies. Even if Isa could of found the key to such a thing, it wouldn't of helped. The past was like guide posts on the high way, receding in the rear view, gone like dust stirred up by the present moment's passing but soon enough to settle. It couldn't ever be brung back. You had to look around at where you were, and try to make sense of the world as best you could with what was in front of your hands.

Out on the cold lonely mountainside. Past the bodies of the unslaved brumbies, dumb and mindless on the slopes now their king was gone. Down through the trees and the scrub into the backroads again. I come to a cross roads and sat to wait for me next ride. I started up a fire and burned Smoov's notes beside the road, watching the embers spark lines of light and the ash drift lighter than air. I took off the trucktyre coat and I was gunna burn that as well but it was cold in the morning light and maybe I would need it for warmth. There wasn't nothing left for me to do but peck at the bodies of Smoov and Isa in me memories so I took out me typewriter to peck at the keys. All the time that new scaled up snake bite skin itched at me wrist and the bigdog robos howled off in the distance and it seemed I was opening up me eyes on the world for the first time or waking up after the dream has bled too long into the morning sunshine and it were a new day ahead to be faced squarely for what it was in its own self and for a tomorrow that would be grown from what we had around us, not the imaginings of what it were like back then. I thought about me dead mum and everything that led up to where I was now and cranked in a fresh sheet of paper and wrote.

About the Author

Andrew Macrae is a typewriter fetishist, a collector of plastic robots and a finder of lost dogs. He plays guitar in The Television Sky, an instrumental rock band based in Melbourne. He also runs his own freelance writing and editing business called Magic Typewriter. *Trucksong* is his first novel, and sprang from a childhood in regional Australia spent listening to the mournful sounds of semi-trailers as they crawled up and down the Great Dividing Range.

Acknowledgements

Cover artwork by Kenkichi Tai: www.kenkichitai.com

Paul Adams, Warren Barker, Deborah Biancotti, Adam Browne, Matthew Chrulew, Rjurik Davidson, Elizabeth Disney, Grace Dugan, Paul Haines, Peter Hickman, Aaron Jacks, Trent Jamieson, Michael Kingston, Tessa Kum, Chris Lawson, the Lee family, Deborah McDonnell, Ben Peek, Cat Sparks, Jeff Sparrow, Keith Stevenson, Fabian Toonen, Kaaron Warren, and Maximillian White.

Visit the *Trucksong* website to download the soundtrack written and performed by Andrew Macrae to accompany the novel.

www.trucksong.com.au

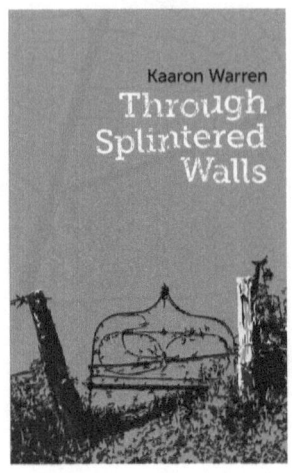

Twelve Planets

Locus Recommended Reading List for Best Collection in 2012

Through Splintered Walls

Kaaron Warren

From Bram Stoker Award nominated author Kaaron Warren, comes Book 6 in the Twelve Planets collection series.

Country road, city street, mountain, creek.
These are stories inspired by the beauty, the danger, the cruelty, emptiness, loneliness and perfection of the Australian landscape.

'Kaaron Warren is a powerful, take-no-prisoners author with an uncanny talent, a deliciously depraved flair for black comedy and a twisted nerve.' —*Alan Kelly*

Twelve Planets

aurealis
awards
FINALIST

Bad Power

Deborah Biancotti

Hate superheroes? Yeah. They probably hate you, too.

'There are two kinds of people with lawyers on tap, Mr Grey. The powerful and the corrupt.'

'Thank you.'

'For implying you're powerful?'

'For imagining those are two different groups.'

From Crawford Award nominee Deborah Biancotti comes this sinister short story suite, a pocketbook police procedural set in a world where the victories are relative and the defeats are absolute. Bad Power celebrates the worst kind of powers both supernatural and otherwise, in the interlinked tales of five people—and how far they'll go.

If you like Haven and Heroes, you'll love Bad Power.

'These appetisingly wicked stories give you the perfect taste of Biancotti's talents.' —*Ann VanderMeer*

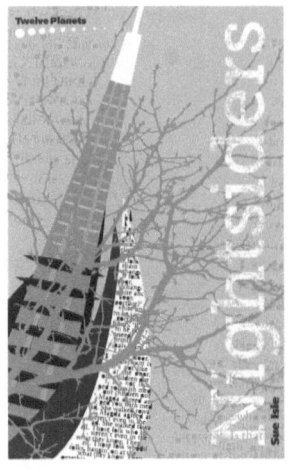

Nightsiders

Sue Isle

In a future world of extreme climate change, the western coast of Australia has been abandoned. A few thousand obstinate, independent souls cling to the southern towns and cities, living mostly by night to endure the fierce temperatures and creating a new culture in defiance of official expectations.

A teenage girl stolen from her family as a child, a troupe of street actors who affects the new with memories of the old, a boy born into the wrong body, and a teacher pushed into the role of guide, all tell the story of The Nightside.

'... [Isle's] writing is uniquely hers, direct and honest and crowned by a deft ear for dialogue.' —Marianne de Pierres

2012 Tiptree Long List Finalist

Locus
Recommended
Reading List for
Best Collection
in 2011

aurealis
awards

FINALIST

Love and Romanpunk

Tansy Rayner Roberts

Thousands of years ago, Julia Agrippina wrote the true history of her family, the Caesars. The document was lost, or destroyed, almost immediately. *(It included more monsters than you might think.)*

Hundreds of years ago, Fanny and Mary ran away from London with a debauched poet and his sister. *(If it was the poet you are thinking of, the story would have ended far more happily, and with fewer people having their throats bitten out.)*

Sometime in the near future, a community will live in a replica Roman city built in the Australian bush. It's a sight to behold. *(Shame about the manticores.)*

Further in the future, the last man who guards the secret history of the world will discover that the past has a way of coming around to bite you. *(He didn't even know she had a thing for pointy teeth.)*

History is not what you think it is.

'Connie Willis meets Gail Carriger over much more than a cup of tea.' —*Helen Merrick*

Winner of the WSFA Small Press Short Story Award

Cracklescape

Margo Lanagan

A presence haunts an old dresser in an inner-city share house. Shining sun-people lure children from their carefree beachside lives. Sheela-na-gigs colonise a middle-aged man's outer and inner worlds. And a girl with a heavy conscience seeks relief in exile on the Treeless Plain.

These stories from four-time World Fantasy Award winner Margo Lanagan are all set in Australia, a myth-soaked landscape both stubbornly inscrutable and crisscrossed by interlopers' dreamings. Explore four littoral and liminal worlds, a-crackle with fears and possibilities.

'Her new collection…may come as something of a revelation even to devoted Lanagan readers.' —*Gary K. Wolfe*

'Margo Lanagan's *Cracklescape* and Kaaron Warren's *Through Splintered Walls* collect four stories apiece, but have more heart and head than many longer books, and feature several of the very best stories of the year.' —*Jonathan Strahan*

Twelve Planets

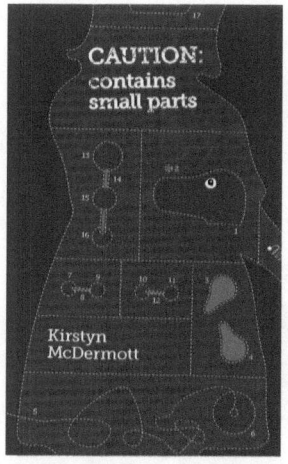

Caution: Contains Small Parts

Kirstyn McDermott

An intimate, unsettling collection from award-winning author Kirstyn McDermott.

A creepy wooden dog that refuses to play dead.

A gifted crisis counsellor and the mysterious, melancholy girl she cannot seem to reach.

A once-successful fantasy author whose life has become a horror story – now with added unicorns.

An isolated woman whose obsession with sex dolls takes a harrowing, unexpected turn.

Four stories that will haunt you long after their final pages are turned.

'Kirstyn McDermott's prose is darkly magical, insidious and insistent. Once her words get under your skin, they are there to stay.'
—*Angela Slatter*

The Company Articles Of Edward Teach

Thoraiya Dyer

Angælien Apocalypse

Matthew Chrulew

A Twelfth Planet Press Double

The Company Articles Of Edward Teach

Learning to live inside your own skin is hard enough, but what if you were thrown back in time, to another body; a different world…?

Angaelien Apocalypse

Reports had come in as the revolution erupted: myriad rotating discs approached Earth at speed. Panic and joy spread around the planet in viral waves. Few needed any help to identify these flying objects. They were the angælic vehicles.

And at the helm of the lead saucer was the Man himself. Jesus Christ.

The Angaelien Apocalypse
Shortlisted for Best SF Short Story, Aurealis Award 2011

The Company Articles of Edward Teach
Winner, Best Novella/Novelette Ditmar 2011

Above *Stephanie Campisi*

Below *Ben Peek*

A Twelfth Planet Press Double

A city has fallen from the sky.

In the wreckage, two men—Devian Lell, a window cleaner in the floating cities of Loft, and Eli Kurran, a security guard in one of the polluted, ground-based cities of Dirt—will find their lives changed.

Devian, who has done what few in the floating landscape have by stepping outside the sanctuary of his home, will be drawn into the politics of Loft, as he is recruited to be the assistant for Dirt's political representative. On the ground, Kurran, still mourning the death of his wife, tries to remove himself from the violent politics of Dirt even as he is blackmailed into providing security for the diplomatic representative of Loft, a woman three times his age, and the oldest living person he has ever met.

A tale of two cities, designed to be self-contained and complete as individual narratives, the two parts can be read in either order, yet also form a single narrative that has been intricately woven and designed to create a single, novel length story. It is a work that suggests not a single way of reading, but rather two, with conflicting morals that will continue to test the reader's certainty in who, in the cities of Loft and Dirt, is in the right.

Roadkill *Robert Shearman*

Siren Beat *Tansy Rayner Roberts*

A Twelfth Planet Press Double

Two novelettes—*Roadkill* by Robert Shearman and *Siren Beat* by Tansy Rayner Roberts—published in tête-bêche format form the first Twelfth Planet Press Double.

Roadkill is a squeamishly uncomfortable story with the kind of illicit weekend away that you never want to have.

Siren Beat is a paranormal romance sans vampires or werewolves but featuring a very sexy sea pony. A minor group of man-eating sirens on the docks of Hobart would not normally pose much of a challenge for Nancy, but she is distracted by the reappearance of Nick Cadmus, the man she blames for her sister's death.

Siren Beat
Winner of the WSFA Small Press Short Story Award
Roadkill
Shortlisted for British Fantasy Award for Best Novella

Horn *Peter M. Ball*

There's a dead girl in a dumpster and a unicorn on the loose. No-one knows how bad that combination can get better than Miriam Aster. What starts as a consulting job for city homicide quickly becomes a tangled knot of unexpected questions, and working out the link between the dead girl and the unicorn will draw Aster back into the world of the exiled fey she thought she'd left behind ten years ago.

Dead girls and unicorns? How warped can this get?

Locus Recommended Reading List

Shortlisted for Best Fantasy Novel and Best Horror Novel, Aurealis Awards

Bleed *Peter M. Ball*

For ten years ex-cop Miriam Aster has been living with her one big mistake—agreeing to kill three men for the exiled Queen of Faerie. But when an old case comes back to haunt her it brings a spectre of the past with it, forcing Aster to ally herself with a stuntwoman and a magic cat in order to rescue a kidnapped TV star from the land of Faerie and stop the half-breed sorcerer who needs Aster's blood.

Shortlisted for the Australian Shadow Award for Best Long Work